THE CHRONICLES OF

AVANTIA

FIRE AND FURY

DISCARD

THE CHRONICLES OF
AVANTIA

THE CHRONICLES OF

AVANTIA

FIRE AND FURY

BY ADAM BLADE

SCHOLASTIC INC.

This book was originally published in hardcover by Scholastic Press in 2013.

ISBN 978-0-545-36153-8

Chronicles of Avantia is a registered trademark of Beast Quest Limited. Series created by Beast Quest Limited, London.

12 11 10 9 8 7 6 5 4 3 2 1   13 14 15 16 17 18/0

Printed in the U.S.A. 40

First Scholastic paperback printing, December 2013

WITH SPECIAL THANKS TO
MICHAEL FORD.

FOR THE TWIN BEASTS,
GABE AND JOEL.

PROLOGUE: FALKOR

*H*ello?" the boy calls. "Can anyone hear me?"

In the darkness, I taste his movements with my flickering tongue. He's not afraid like the others, though he should be. The caves have many turns, many dead ends that swallow up the light. The creatures that come in here for warmth or shelter stumble or flap among the rocks until they're completely lost. Some talk to themselves; some sob as terror closes its fist around their hearts. I take them silently, sliding across the ground and seizing them in my coils. Their cries die quickly, leaving only echoes.

"Hello?" he whispers. "Issy, are you in here?"

The boy's footsteps scuff nearby. Snout first, I drift like a deadly breeze toward him. My scales grip the cold rock and push me onward. My fangs sing with anticipation of my next meal.

There he is! A young boy. The burned-out torch in his hand trails a gray plume of smoke; it led me straight to him. These humans never learn! He has his back to me, so I thread around a boulder and slither on my belly toward him. I lift my head from the ground, ready to strike.

My movement disturbs a trickle of stones, and he turns, gasps, and staggers backward to the wall of the cavern. He holds his shepherd's crook across his chest as our eyes meet. But what's this? Something stops me from delivering the lethal blow.

It cannot be.

Along the sinuous coils of my body, a new feeling stirs. New, yet ancient: fossilized into the very fiber of my being. It's him! The one who is chosen for me.

I lower my head, edging closer to him, seeking his scent with my forked tongue. His breath comes in pants. As I bring my head to his level, I see the reflection of myself in his wide eyes. The blunt head, my forked, darting tongue.

I still expect him to scream, or cry, but instead he lowers the crook and smiles.

"Hello," he says.

His human eyes aren't good enough to see, but my scales glow pink, deepening to red, scarlet, indigo: Greetings, young one.

Tentatively, he reaches out a hand and places it on my snout. His skin is warm, but there's more than hot blood flowing through this boy's veins. Something older, and more powerful, lurks within him.

"I'm Rufus," he whispers.

I hiss, rippling yellows and greens. Falkor.

He frowns, then repeats, "Falkor."

He hears me. There can be no doubt: He's my Chosen One.

Come, follow me, I say.

I twist away from him, gliding across the cave toward the only exit that leads to safety. He comes behind me, one hand resting on my scales to guide him. I check back from time to time, but this boy seems unfazed to be sharing the gloom with a Beast that towers over him.

Soon, we reach the cave's ragged mouth. I've become so used to the darkness that the daylight hurts my eyes. The Cave of Bones, that's what the villagers called it years ago. How quickly they forget. Until today, I was just a myth, a story told to frighten children.

Rufus rushes ahead, out into the light, and as the fire recedes from my eyes I see the grassy slopes of Avantia stretching far away. Sheep are scattered in the fields, and hunger forms a knot in my stomach. For years I've dwelled in the darkness, but that time is at an end. The age of the Beasts approaches once more.

"There you are!" calls a voice. My scales stiffen and I jerk my head toward it. A girl-child stands with her hands on her hips. Around her neck, a water flagon hangs on a strap. Though her hair is darker than the boy's, I taste their common blood — she is his sister. Rufus glances at me, his face creased with worry, and I slink back into the shadows. I understand: Though he is unafraid, my presence would alarm his kin.

"Where've you been?" she asks, climbing the slope toward the cave entrance.

"I was looking for you, Isadora," he says.

"There's no way I'd hide in there," she says. "I waited in the hollow of an oak tree. Father would be furious if he found out you'd been in the Cave of Bones."

"Well, don't tell him, then," said Rufus.

From my hiding place, I see the girl fold her arms across her chest. "Why shouldn't I?"

4

Rufus slides down the gravel slope toward her. "I'll show you a trick if you don't."

"It had better be a good one," she says.

He points to a rock ten paces away. "Put your water flagon on there."

His sister does as he asks. "Now what?"

"I bet you I can smash it to pieces without going anywhere near it," he says.

She laughs. "You must think I'm stupid."

"Stand back," says Rufus, suddenly serious.

His sister steps away from the rock, shaking her head, and Rufus lowers his shepherd's crook, pointing it at the flask. The mountain air seems to still, yet is abuzz with power. His eyes, unblinking, focus along the staff. I see his knuckles whiten and his arm tremble. That strange feeling in the cave, when he placed his hand on my scales, now touches me again.

A bolt of white light blasts from his fingertips, scorching the air. My scales ripple with the shock of it, and I narrow my eyes against the glare. The girl screams. When my vision clears, Rufus has fallen onto his rear, though he still clutches the crook. The flagon rests, undamaged, on the rock. But behind it, a sapling smolders, its trunk split into two charred splints, its leaves ablaze. My tongue finds the taste of boiling sap.

"Missed!" says Rufus.

On the slope, the sheep have fled through a far gate.

"But . . . that's amazing!" squeals his sister, mesmerized by the burning tree. "How did you do that?"

Rufus finds his feet again and hands his sister back her flagon. "I don't know." He shrugs. "It just happened a few weeks ago. I've been practicing."

The girl throws her arms around him. "One day you'll be a great wizard," she says. "Like in the stories about men fighting Beasts."

Rufus laughs. "Well, I don't know about that," he says. He looks over his sister's shoulder, straight at me. I let my scales turn all the colors of the rainbow, and he grins. "You shouldn't believe all the stories, sister," he says. "Everyone knows that Beasts aren't real."

As the ashes from the charred leaves drift across the ground, she wants him to perform the trick again.

"I'm not sure I can," he says. "It makes me tired."

"Tomorrow, then?"

"Maybe. But listen, Issy, you have to promise not to tell anyone. If someone in Hartwell finds out, I'll get a thrashing, or worse."

I hiss at the thought of it, and my scales take on a fiery red hue.

No one will hurt my Chosen Rider. Not while Falkor has venom in his fangs.

CHAPTER 1

*T*he thick clouds make the sky the color of steel. Lightning flashes above and thunder growls like a giant woken from sleep. Cold needles of rain drive against my wings as I soar over forest and plain. Yet the water doesn't chill me. Nothing can quench the ever-burning fire of a phoenix.

I've watched the sun loop across the sky three times since our battle with Derthsin's minions: the dragon-helmeted General Gor and his Beast, Varlot. Still I hear the sound of clashing metal and war cries beneath the walls of the ruined castle, still I smell the fear of men in my feathers, and still I taste their blood on my beak.

Nera unfolds her long stride below us, her ears flattened and amber eyes flashing. Her sodden fur ripples gold and brown under the lightning that illuminates the plain.

Between her shoulder blades Castor crouches, his hands gripping her fur. At my side, Gulkien stirs the mists in great drafts with his wings of bone and stretched skin. Droplets of spray scatter from his bristling gray coat, and his long nostrils flare as they suck in damp air. He carries the fair-haired girl, Gwen. Her face is set hard and her eyes are narrowed to slits against the elements. In the recesses of the cloak that whips and flaps around her, the silver of her throwing axes glitters.

The weight on my own back shifts a fraction as Tanner grips my flanks tighter with his knees. How long is it that we have flown together, my Chosen Rider and I? I feel his heartbeat as if it were the pulse of my own hot blood. The bond was between us even before the day when Derthsin slew Tanner's parents. Our bond was forged in the fires of the past, when Fate decreed the Beasts of Avantia should each have a Chosen Rider. But now we are closer than we have ever been before — my blood flows in Tanner's veins, after he drank from the vial given to him by the medicine woman. Pain twists deep inside me. He should never have done that! But it is too late now; he is changing, an unnatural *strength pumping through his veins. He now thinks he's unstoppable.*

Tanner lays the flat of his palm gently against the feathers on my back, and I hear his voice, somewhere deep in the fibers of my being.

Can we trust him?

I know the one of whom he speaks and tip my head to gaze at the fourth of our number — the final companion — who we have known for the shortest time. Falkor slithers as fast as Nera runs, his long serpent's body pulsing between the tall grasses, his tongue tasting the air. His scales, slick with moisture, shimmer purple, black, and blue. As he plunges into a dense patch of forest, I have a brief glimpse of the newest rider, seated behind the jutting spines on my fellow Beast's head, the one whose loyalty Tanner doubts — Rufus. He holds the pieces of the mask that were handed over to him by Tanner. Up till now, he's kept the pieces in the lining of his cloak, safe from prying eyes. But can we keep our faith in him?

Time will tell, *I answer.*

Falkor has chosen him, as I have chosen Tanner and the others have been drawn to their mortal companions. I should not question another Beast.

Tanner sends more words to me. We should land, Firepos.

With a screech, I dip my wings to bring us into a long glide downward. The forest blurs as my talons rip through the upper branches. A clearing rushes toward us.

Yes, time will tell.

The rain had finally stopped. Fat droplets of water hung from every leaf tip like crystals. Spokes of sunlight slipped through the canopy and lit up patches of mossy ground. Tanner carried two dead rabbits over his shoulder and leaped over a fallen, rotting trunk, feeling his muscles ache after the recent battles. Only three days before they'd faced General Gor's troops in the ruins of the mountaintop castle over the Southern Caves. They'd won a victory of sorts, driving Gor away.

They had claimed three pieces of the Mask of Death, but carrying the fragments put their lives in more danger than ever.

Evil gripped the scattered towns and villages of Avantia in its iron fist. Tanner couldn't forget the attack on his home village of Forton, or General Gor's twisted sneer as he'd called his troops back from the scene of their latest fight at the ruined castle. *You can't win!* he'd jeered, his varkule carrying him away. Perhaps he was right. The warlord Derthsin's rage would be boundless in his quest for the fourth and final piece of the mask — the Face of Anoret. If he succeeded, Tanner knew that power over all the Beasts would fall to the wearer: Derthsin.

That can't happen, Tanner thought. *I cannot put myself and my friends through this for nothing.*

Thoughts of the mask brought a wave of dizziness, and Tanner had to steady himself against the trunk of a tree. He'd only worn the broken mask for a few moments, but he'd felt the power that lurked within it. If only he could trust himself to use the power wisely. Perhaps the Mask of Death could be a force for good, perhaps . . .

"No!" he said aloud, shaking his head to clear the thoughts.

He rested his forehead against the tree, letting the rich scents of the earth and plants soothe him.

The mask is a curse. All that matters is keeping it from Derthsin.

Closing his eyes, he could almost imagine that Avantia was at peace. The forest smell reminded him of the woods near his old home in Forton — of his grandmother, Esme, chopping wood in front of the cottage. His eyes snapped open. But Esme, brave and proud to the end, had been cruelly cut down by General Gor.

If only I'd fought harder, Tanner thought angrily. *Maybe I could have saved her.*

He stroked the red scrap of linen around his wrist — torn from his grandmother's body as a memento of that day, a blood-colored token of unfinished business. Of revenge.

If you used the mask, vengeance would be easy. . . .

Tanner swallowed. Was the voice inside his head even his anymore? Or did some dark part of him lust after power like Derthsin? Too much time alone; too much thinking. He pushed a strand of wet hair from his face and retraced his steps back up to the caves. Soon his nostrils picked up the smell of smoke. Good!

At least the others had managed to find enough dry wood to get a fire going.

As the leaves ahead parted, Firepos pushed through her golden beak and cawed softly. Her yellow eyes relaxed when she saw that he was safe. Tanner reached up to stroke the warm, soft feathers beneath her head.

"It's all right, I'm back," he said. He held up the rabbits. "With supper."

She called softly again, ruffling her glorious wings. Anxiety sent a ripple of low flames across her feathers. Tanner broke eye contact. Since he'd been tricked into drinking a vial of Firepos's blood, something had changed between them. He remembered how it had felt:

The red liquid trickles down my throat. I wipe a hand across my mouth and Gwen's eyes widen in horror as she points at my fingers. Streaked with blood! Almost instantly, I feel my veins burn with energy coursing through them. I have a Beast's bravery and strength for battle. I squeeze my eyes tight shut as a sensation close to pain sweeps over me. Then my eyes snap open as I

realize: Something has changed within me. Some-
thing has gone badly wrong.

Tanner pushed the memory of that moment away. He
and Firepos were closer than ever — he'd drunk his
Beast's blood! It had given him a Beast's strength, but
in turn that had been twisted into a vicious bloodlust
after he'd tried on a piece of the mask. Tanner knew
that danger hovered around him. Was it enough to
jeopardize their mission?

Stay strong, my rider, came Firepos's voice.

"We're only four mortals and four Beasts," muttered Tanner.

It's enough, said Firepos.

Tanner straightened his shoulders as he emerged
by the black boulder near the dark hollow of the cave
mouth. Nera, resting on her golden haunches, jerked
her head up with a flash of her orange eyes. Her hack-
les rose and she sent out a growl as she watched him
cross the cave. Gulkien, always more friendly, yawned
to reveal curved fangs as long as Tanner's forearm, his
flanks rising and falling slowly.

As Tanner passed them, Nera snapped with her drooling jaws at the rabbits.

"Get off!" laughed Tanner, pushing the massive head away. Typical of Castor's Beast to try to take what wasn't hers. "Fetch your own dinner."

Nera snarled, and Tanner quickened his steps into the cave.

He almost didn't see Falkor, coiled up and watching him, half in the shade cast by the lip of the cave, half basking in the sunlight. The Beast lay still as a fossil but for the blink of one diamond-shaped eye. His tongue flickered out in a kind of greeting.

The smell of smoke was stronger here, and spluttering flames lit up the interior of the cave where Gwen, Castor, and Rufus had gathered around the fire, drying themselves after the storm.

Castor, lying on his back with his head resting on his arms, turned toward Tanner.

"About time you showed up," he said. "We're starving here."

Tanner rolled his eyes. "I don't remember you volunteering to catch dinner," he replied.

"I wish I had," said the boy from Colton. "We'd have eaten hours ago."

"Enough, you two," said Gwen, standing up from the fire. "We need to eat quickly. Derthsin won't wait. Pass me your dagger, Rufus."

Rufus handed her the knife hilt-first. She took the rabbits from Tanner and immediately went to work, skinning them expertly.

Rufus left the fireside and went to sit near the back of the cave, draping his blue tunic over his knees. His staff was leaning against the wall and the firelight picked out the carvings of scales along its length, ending in the head of a serpent. The curved blade fixed to the top gleamed. Tanner didn't know whether to trust him, but Falkor obviously did. The wizard boy was a Chosen Rider, like the rest of them.

Rufus cast a handful of rattling bone pieces onto the hard-packed ground in front of him. He leaned forward, peering at them. Tanner felt a pang of homesickness and the dull ache of grief. His grandmother had also been a mystic, looking for the future in the patterns of rune stones.

"Where'd you find the bones?" Tanner asked.

Rufus looked up sharply. "Falkor sniffed them out. Animal bones, I suppose, picked clean by vultures." He quickly pushed them aside and pulled out a small wooden box from inside his jerkin. Opening it, he took out a pinch of brown fibers and held them flat on his palm. His lips mumbled words Tanner couldn't hear.

Nothing happened.

"That's very impressive," Castor called over, sneering.

Rufus shot him an angry look and returned his attention to his palm, chanting again. Flames leaped from the fibers, then died. He grinned to himself.

"Magician's tricks," Castor grumbled.

Gwen skinned and gutted the first rabbit swiftly, tossing the entrails to Gulkien, who snatched them up with bloodstained jaws. Before she could start the second, Castor grabbed the dagger from her hand.

"Hurry up, will you?" he said. He began to hack at the carcass.

"What are you doing?" Rufus said. "There'll be no meat worth eating!"

Castor dropped the rabbit at Gwen's feet. "Calm down, Rufus. Not everyone's been as lucky as you, living in a cave and skinning rats," he said.

Rufus's eyes darkened. "Well, at least Gwen knows what she's doing."

Castor sniffed. "Too bad she's busy daydreaming about her traitor brother."

Tanner saw Gwen flush, but instead of attacking Castor, she drifted across the cave with her arms folded in front of her. Even a week ago, she'd have lunged for him. *Something's changed in her*, Tanner thought.

It wasn't surprising after everything she'd been through — the death of her brother, his return as a living corpse, his final fall from the cliff. Tanner glared at Castor and went after her. She gazed out toward the Avantian horizon with its scattering of villages and fields. There were no strict boundaries, or hadn't been until the arrival of Derthsin. Now every town and village, however small, had a line of defense.

Tanner saw tears sparkling in the corners of Gwen's eyes.

"He's just being Castor," he whispered. "He doesn't mean it. You know what he's like."

"He's right, though, isn't he?" she said sadly, looking at the ground. "Geffen did betray us."

Tanner put his arm around his friend, unsure of
what to say. Gwen's twin brother had been kidnapped
by General Gor, who'd thought he held the secrets of
Jonas the Mapmaker. Gor had been wrong — Jonas
had confided his knowledge to Gwen instead. Tanner
and the riders had managed to rescue Geffen but he'd
abandoned them, stealing a piece of the mask and falling under the evil sway of Gor and his leader, Derthsin.
The boy had made a terrible mistake and had paid a
terrible price: brought back to life as a fighting
corpse — an undead soldier. Only by taking his own
life had he ended the curse. Gwen had watched her
brother throw himself from a cliff ledge.

"At least he's not suffering anymore," said Tanner.

Gwen looked up. "I wish I could understand what
happened to him," she said. "I keep asking myself:
Why would Derthsin do such a thing?"

"He wanted to hurt you," he said. "Hurt all of us."
Tanner squeezed his eyes tight shut for a moment.
He would never forget the green, rotting flesh
peeling from Geffen's bones. "What better way than

by using the person dearest to you? But you must stay strong, Gwen. Show him that his games won't defeat you."

She smiled thinly, her shoulders sagging. Tanner reached for Gwen's belt and pulled her rapier, with the hilt like a wolf's head, from its sheath. Dried blood still streaked the blade from their last battle.

"You have to clean it," Tanner said. "Otherwise it will rust."

Gwen's fingers tightened around the hilt. "For Geffen," she said grimly. She embraced Tanner in a quick hug. "Thank you."

"What a touching little scene," sneered Castor from the cave.

Tanner broke away from Gwen. "Stop it, Castor."

But Castor was on his feet now, kicking the rabbit fur out of the way. He brushed the blond locks from his face and took a couple of steps toward Tanner. "Very convenient, isn't it?" he said. "No one seems to be pointing the finger of blame."

Tanner gritted his teeth. *Don't get angry.*

"Blame for what?" asked Rufus, picking up the rabbits and continuing to skin them.

Castor shrugged his muscular shoulders. "For letting Gor get away, of course. If Tanner had killed him in that battle in the castle ruins, maybe Geffen wouldn't have attacked Gwen. Maybe . . ." He paused. "Maybe he could have been saved."

Tanner glared at Castor, his feet rooted to the ground even though every sinew wanted to explode. *Stay calm, stay calm* . . . Ever since Tanner had put the piece of the mask over his face, he seemed less able to control his anger.

"That's not fair," snapped Gwen. "There's no saying what might have happened."

Castor took a few more cocky steps closer, arms spread wide, never taking his eyes off Tanner. He jabbed a finger in Tanner's direction. "I'm surprised our fortune-teller here didn't foresee it. He's had one vision from wearing the mask — or so he *says*."

Don't fight him, called Firepos.

But it was too late. Tanner's anger finally boiled over. How dare Castor mock his premonition about the death of a Beast? With a cry, he threw himself at Castor.

CHAPTER 2

*O*_{ooo}!

Tanner pushed Castor against the cave wall, then drew back his fist and punched. His knuckles smashed into Castor's cheekbone, and Castor howled in pain. Tanner punched again, but Castor ducked underneath the blow and Tanner's hand hit the wall. Pain flared across his scuffed fingers. Castor slipped a foot behind Tanner's leg and tripped him backward, but Tanner grabbed Castor's tunic collar and they fell together in a tangle of limbs.

"I'll kill you!" shouted Castor. His Beast hissed, lips peeled back from her fangs. Firepos flapped her huge wings, sending out curls of fire from her rainbow feathers.

Tanner managed to get his hands around Castor's throat and pressed all his weight on the other boy's chest. "I'd like to see you try!" he shouted.

Control yourself, came Firepos's angry message. Tanner could hardly bear to listen.

"Stop it!" said Gwen.

Castor punched Tanner, and he fell sideways with a grunt. Castor staggered up and drew back his leg to kick Tanner, but Tanner lashed out with his foot, catching Castor's knee. Castor sucked in a breath and backed off, clutching his leg. He crashed into Rufus, knocking the rabbits into the fire.

"Great!" shouted Rufus. "Now you've ruined dinner!"

Tanner clambered to his feet, flexing his fists. He noticed that Falkor had lifted his head on his scaly neck, watching them both.

"Had enough?" Tanner said to Castor.

Castor wiped his nose, streaking blood across his cheek. "What do you think?"

He ran at Tanner, swinging a fist, but Tanner caught his arm and twisted, hoisting Castor off his feet. Castor's momentum pulled Tanner down, too, and they rolled together out of the cave. Castor lashed out with his fist, catching Tanner's temple and making him reel. He punched blindly and heard Castor grunt. Tanner's eyes swam into focus. Castor was clutching his stomach, doubled over.

"That all you've got?" hissed Castor.

Tanner jumped up. *Time to finish this.* Something seized his collar. He turned. "Gwen! Let me . . ."

Not Gwen. Firepos had his tunic gripped firmly in her beak. She yanked him back, and he landed in the mud with a splat. Tanner looked up into her blazing eyes. "Why'd you do that?" As if he had to ask. He suddenly felt clumsy and stupid, shame burning his cheeks.

Castor laughed and picked up a piece of charred firewood, glowing orange at one end and trailing sparks. As he took a step toward Tanner, a dark shadow landed almost noiselessly between them. Nera nudged Castor with her foreleg. As he stumbled back, she turned to Tanner and snarled, revealing her daggerlike fangs. Then she twisted to Castor and growled menacingly. Firepos let out a soft caw.

Enough.

Castor dropped the piece of wood. "It's lucky your Beast came to protect you," he said, stalking back into the cave. Inside, Tanner saw Gwen shaking her head as Rufus tried to rescue what he could of the rabbits from the fire.

Tanner sat up, letting air cool his skin and the fury that boiled beneath. His fist was red, both with his own blood where he'd cut his knuckles and Castor's. A wave of revulsion swept through him, taking the last of his anger with it. *What's gotten into me?* he thought.

Firepos lowered her head and brushed his shoulder with her beak. Tanner knew *exactly* what had infected him. *It's not just Firepos's blood. It's the mask, too.* Knowing that the three pieces were in Rufus's cape made the hot fever coursing through his veins move even faster. He wanted to put them on, fight anyone who dared approach — spill their blood. *Even my friends*, he thought, shame tearing through him.

Tanner put a hand on the tawny feathers behind Firepos's head and heaved himself to his feet.

The hatred that fogs his mind has gone, snatched away like clouds by the breeze. His eyes meet mine, full of remorse. Yes, I understand, Tanner. You only wore a fragment of the Mask of Death, but the Face of Anoret holds a power that infects the mind and fills the wearer with bloodlust.

You must fight its power if you are to wear it again, especially now that my blood flows in your veins. My power, combined with the bloodlust of the Mask of Death, could be disastrous for Avantia.

Listen, and listen carefully, companion of mine: Your mind is tainted, but it is still your own. The boy Castor is your friend, though it may not seem so now. Stay strong, Chosen Rider. Without you, our journey will be for nothing.

Does Tanner hear me? He may be too full of fury to listen.

Tanner had closed his mind to Firepos. *Just for now,* he told himself. *I need to think straight.* He walked back into the cave and found Castor poking the fire aimlessly with a stick. Gwen and Rufus watched him closely. He held out his hand.

"Sorry," he said. "We're all tired."

Castor looked at the hand and snorted.

Tanner didn't have any anger left. "If we don't stick together, we'll be letting down all those who've died. My grandmother Esme, Geffen, the people of Colton, Forton, and Hartwell. Those boys in the mines . . ."

My parents.

He remembered Derthsin's sword sliding between his father's ribs, his mother's screams as the soldiers dragged her away.

We've lost so much, he thought. Would he ever see his mother again? He wasn't even sure he could remember her face. Would he recognize her if he did meet her?

Castor turned from the fire, his face flushed, and took Tanner's hand. He gave a small nod. "We should eat."

The charred rabbit was tough as boot leather, but Tanner felt better having some meat in his belly. As Rufus kicked over the embers of the fire, they each settled down to sleep. Stars twinkled overhead. Tanner could feel the night getting colder with each passing moment.

Tomorrow we travel, he told himself. *Tomorrow, it begins again.*

Gwen unrolled the map of the kingdom and smoothed its dry, cracked edges flat. The four friends gathered around in the dim gray light of dawn as she opened her locket. The folded gossamer, as light as a butterfly's wing, seemed to fall open like a shimmering cloud, so thin it was almost invisible but for a diamond sparkle where it caught the light. It billowed even with the softest touch of their breath, and she laid it flat over the map. Tanner felt Firepos's shadow move over him, and Falkor coiled inside the cave to focus the dark pools of his eyes on the map. Gulkien crept closer with Nera at his side, until all four Beasts stood watching patiently with their riders.

As Gwen shifted the gossamer into position, the surface of the map blurred and then became clear before Tanner's eyes: the kingdom sprinkled with a thousand details: ridges, valleys, fields, and roads. The sea, lapping against the western shore, seemed almost alive. Names, scored in tiny, perfect lettering, appeared across the terrain.

"Look!" said Rufus, pointing a trembling finger toward the east of the kingdom.

For a moment, Tanner's eyes fixed on the bulk inside Rufus's blue cloak — the three pieces of the mask.

"Tanner?" said Castor.

Tanner tore his gaze to where Rufus was pointing, and his heart thumped in his chest when he saw where the final piece of the mask had appeared.

"It's by the great volcano," said Gwen.

"That's where Firepos almost killed Derthsin, years ago," Tanner said. "Where it all began. Where Derthsin should have died." His eyes fell on the word "Forton," spelled out in tiny letters not far from the volcano's slopes. "Near my home, too."

"Geffen's seen . . . saw . . . the map as well," said Castor. "He would have told General Gor or Vendrake where the mask is."

"They might be heading there already," added Rufus, using his staff to stand up.

Tanner felt a wave of exhaustion. Castor was right. And Derthsin had a whole army at his disposal, rearmed and re-energized. He shuddered at the thought of the massed black-clad ranks, the riders on drooling, snapping varkules thirsty for blood. How could the four of them defeat a force that size, even with their Beasts? But he kept his thoughts to himself as he looked at his friends. Their hopes need kindling, not drowning with despair.

As he turned, he saw that Rufus had moved to sit a few paces away, near the mouth of the cave. He cast a handful of the rattling bone pieces onto the ground, and peered at the scatter with a smile. Tanner had given up trying to see a pattern in them. They were as impossible for him to read as Esme's rune stones had been.

When Rufus saw him looking, he snatched up the bones and turned his back. As he did so, one of the three pieces of the mask fell out of his cloak.

Tanner jumped forward and snatched it up. The section was from the upper right side of Anoret's face, rough with ridges and hardened scales. Tanner turned it over and stroked his fingers across the smooth, pelt-like inner surface.

Rufus held out his hand. "Better if I look after it," he said.

Tanner drew back. "Yes," he said, but he clutched it to his chest. The hollow eye socket of the mask locked him in a hollow stare. *I could put it on. . . .*

"Give it to me, Tanner," said Rufus.

I could wear it again. I could take a swift revenge. . . .

Give it back, said Firepos. Distracted, Tanner had allowed his mind to open up to his Beast again. The flame bird's voice broke through Tanner's muddled thoughts. He held out the fragment, and Rufus snatched it back, staring hard at Tanner.

"Don't worry," he said, giving a brittle smile. "I'll keep it safe."

"Are we going or not?" asked Castor. He tied on his sword belt and marched out of the cave, seemingly oblivious to the tension.

Tanner helped Gwen roll up the map. "We have to stick together," she said. Her voice was soft but firm. *Did she realize what was happening there? Does she know how I feel?* Tanner felt sick to his stomach at the treacherous thoughts flooding him one moment, only for him to find the strength to push them away the next. *What type of person have I become?*

You're a brave fighter, Firepos reassured him. *With a good heart. Don't forget that.*

"Don't worry," Tanner told Gwen, trying to control the tremor in his voice. "We will."

As he took up his sword from the side of the cave, feeling its familiar weight around his hips, Tanner's weariness slipped away. Firepos's words had done their job; they'd made him feel better about himself. The sky had blushed to pink as the first rays of morning sun trickled through the trees. Outside the cave, Castor already sat astride Nera, and the massive cat was padding down toward the trees. *Typical,* thought Tanner with a wry smile. *He never waits for anyone!*

Firepos screeched and lowered a wing for Tanner to climb up. He settled into her warm feathers. "Time to fly again, old friend," he said. He brought his face down close to her head. "Thank you," he whispered.

With a hiss, Falkor slithered past the cave entrance,

following in Nera's tracks. Rufus was astride his back. Gulkien growled and leaped up onto a boulder, gripping the rock with his claws and flexing his leathery wings.

"Let's not get separated," Gwen said to Tanner, climbing onto her Beast's back. "Take us up, Gulkien," she said.

The air wolf bent his powerful rear legs and leaped into the sky. With two heaves of his wings, Gulkien climbed over the cave.

Firepos lifted her wings and sprang up. As she rose above their campsite, Tanner's heart filled with a mixture of exhilaration and dread. The rain had stopped completely, and a rainbow arced in the distance over the great plains. Beyond it, the sky looked black and stormy; the weather could change at any moment.

Firepos flew up in a tight spiral into the thin shreds of cloud that remained. Tanner leaned close to her warm feathers as a chill morning breeze ruffled his clothes. He tried to forget about the mask.

As Firepos wheeled around to fly after Gulkien, Tanner peered over his Beast's side. Beneath them, Nera slunk between the trees and flashes of Falkor's glittering scales became visible as he slithered through the forest. Tanner's hand traveled down Firepos's body and found the bare patch of scarred skin beneath her wing. It was an old scar she carried from her battle with Derthsin, when she dropped him into the volcano, his hand still clutching one of her feathers. Somehow, Derthsin had survived. It was almost as if their destinies were connected, and now Tanner had drunk the flame bird's blood, the threads of their three lives seemed more entwined than ever. Derthsin had spilled Firepos's blood and Tanner had drunk it. And all of this had happened because Derthsin wanted the Mask of Death to control the Beasts of Avantia for his own evil ends.

Firepos put on a burst of speed. Exhilaration flooded Tanner's veins. *I won't be cowed!* No matter what pain the past had brought, together they could end the curse that covered Avantia like a black shroud.

Gwen looked back and smiled. Tanner waved, but her smile changed quickly to a frown. She pulled on Gulkien's fur and the wolf tipped his wings, slowing until Firepos and Tanner flew up alongside them.

"What is it?" Tanner called over.

Gwen pointed back the way they'd come. "I thought I saw a movement in the mouth of the cave we just left. It looked like a person."

"You're sure?" he asked.

She nodded. Tanner looked as well, but could see nothing. "Firepos, call to the others. We need to stop."

As the flame bird dipped her wings, dropping down to a patch of high, rocky ground, she let out a series of short caws. Nera and Falkor changed direction and the Beasts gathered on the rocks. Nera's pink tongue hung from her mouth as Castor slipped off her back. "What's going on, Tanner? Your Beast tired already?"

"Gwen thought she saw someone, back at the cave," Tanner said, ignoring Castor's remark.

Castor squinted. "Well, *I* can't see anything!"

Rufus shrugged. "Me neither."

Would Derthsin really send scouts to track them, when he had whole armies at his disposal? It didn't seem likely, but Tanner trusted Gwen more than anyone.

"We shouldn't take any risks," he said. "Let's encircle the camp and close in."

Rufus and Gwen nodded, and Castor sighed. "If we must. But we're never going to get anywhere if we don't push on."

They mounted their Beasts again. "I'll come from the rear," said Tanner. "Gwen, take the front approach; Castor and Rufus, come from the sides."

"How come Gwen gets the direct attack?" said Castor.

"It's not an attack," said Tanner, "until we know it's an enemy." He wouldn't share his fears with the others yet.

He tugged on Firepos's feathers, and the flame bird lifted off the rocks, swooping low over the trees with her wing tips rustling the leaves; no one at ground level would see her coming. Tanner checked back to see Falkor slicing through the undergrowth and Nera padding silently, fanning out in opposite directions. Gulkien, with his wings folded into his sides, took long strides on his massive paws.

Tanner guided Firepos wide of the campsite, then looped around the back. With one hand on his Beast's feathers, Tanner let his other drop to the hilt of his sword. Firepos thrust out her talons and landed above the cave entrance. From the rustle of the trees on both sides, Tanner knew that Falkor and Nera must be closing in, too.

A cry split the air from the forest behind him. It was Gwen.

CHAPTER 3

Falkor and Nera burst from the trees on either side of Tanner, who pointed in the direction of the cry. "Find Gwen!" he called to Rufus and Castor. "Hurry!"

Tanner squeezed with his thighs and Firepos jumped into the air, gliding down toward the forest. His stomach twisted with anxiety. *I shouldn't have split us up*, he thought. *If something's happened to her . . .*

As the flame bird neared the ground, Tanner slipped from her side, landing neatly and rolling to his feet. Barely breaking stride, he plunged into the trees, drawing his sword.

"Gwen!" he called. "Where are you?"

"I can see Gulkien!" shouted Castor's voice somewhere to his right.

Tanner stumbled over a tree root and caught sight of movement ahead. A large, hooded man clutched Gwen around the middle and hoisted her off the ground.

"Let go of her!" he shouted.

Gwen twisted, eyes wide. Tanner sprinted at them, raising his sword ready to strike. He heard a snarl, and Gulkien pounced into view. With a flick of his leathery wing, he sent Tanner sprawling across the mossy ground. The wolf stood over him. As Tanner climbed to his feet, Gwen half turned. Instead of anguish or terror, Tanner caught the curl of a smile.

Tanner looked between Gwen and her attacker. "I don't understand," he said.

"That's enough, Gulkien," Gwen whispered, slipping from the man's arms. "Tanner wasn't to know."

"What . . . ? Who . . . ?" Tanner began.

The man stepped beside Gwen. He wore a filthy cloak over his broad shoulders, stained and torn, with sections of different material stitched over old rips and holes. He pulled back his brown hood to reveal weather-beaten features, tanned and weary. It was difficult to tell how old he was, so deep were the furrows etched into his brow. The lower half of his face was covered in a shaggy yellow beard. His hair was gray and thinning on top, but as he turned to Gwen and put his arm around her, Tanner saw he had tied the long strands of hair back and threaded them with beads. *Like my grandmother*, Tanner thought. Despite his haggard appearance, the old man's brown eyes shone.

"I'm Jonas," he said in a deep voice.

The name set off a spark in Tanner's brain. Jonas? "The mapmaker!" he gasped.

With her dying words, Esme had sent Tanner looking for Jonas, but when he'd arrived in the mapmaker's town, the man was long gone, leaving behind the twins he'd rescued and raised as children: Gwen and Geffen.

"Is it really *you*?" asked Gwen, taking Jonas's hand. "I . . . I can't believe it."

At that moment, Nera pounced into the clearing, teeth bared, and from the opposite side, Rufus ducked under a branch on Falkor's back. The man shrank away.

Castor jumped down from Nera's fur and drew his dagger. "Get away from her!" he shouted, running at the man.

"No!" Gwen said, slapping the dagger away. "Jonas is my . . . He looked after Geffen and me when we were young."

"Well, what's he doing here?" asked Castor.

"Don't be so rude!" snapped Gwen.

Castor ignored her. "Well?" he demanded, frowning at the mapmaker.

They stood in a circle, gazing at each other, as swallows darted overhead. What *was* this man doing here? Tanner had seen too many attacks on villages and innocent deaths to believe in coincidence anymore. Everything happened in Avantia for a reason — and usually that reason was evil.

"It's a long story," Jonas said eventually.

"Not good enough," Castor snapped.

For once, Tanner thought that Castor was right. It was only the hurt in Gwen's eyes that stopped him from flinging his own questions at the mapmaker. A message throbbed through the air to him from Firepos. *Stay calm. Move slowly. The truth will reveal itself.*

"The morning's almost over already," said Rufus, turning his back on Jonas to address his friends. His face was mottled with red patches of agitation. "We should be halfway to the volcano by now!"

Gwen gently pushed Rufus away. "Give me a moment," she said. Her eyes pleaded with them. "There's something I must say."

She knelt at the mapmaker's feet and pulled him down to sit on a stone. She grasped his gnarled hands in hers, and Tanner's heart ached to see that his fingers were twisted with age. He probably couldn't even hold a quill now, much less make maps.

"It's Geffen," she said, gazing up into the man's face. Silver crescents of tears brimmed in her eyes. "He's . . ." She lowered her face to the ground, her voice thick with emotion.

Pain creased the old man's face. "I know," he said softly.

Alarm darted through Tanner's body.

"How do you know?" he demanded. The words were out before he could stop them, and Gwen threw him a furious glance.

"I move from town to village, sleeping where I

can," Jonas said, his eyes narrowing. "You'd be surprised at how much I hear and the pain it can cause." His eyes welled with tears, but he brushed them away. He turned back to Gwen. "I've been looking for you since I heard Colweir was in trouble," said Jonas. "But I was always one step behind. It's hard when you have these magnificent creatures and I'm on foot."

"All this time you were near us," Gwen said. "I felt it, I'm sure."

Tanner pulled her aside. "Something doesn't feel right," he whispered. "Jonas left you years ago. Why's he turned up now, when we've got some of the mask? Have you asked yourself why? Are you thinking straight, Gwen?"

Gwen swallowed, and a cloud of pain crossed over her face. "That's a horrible thing to say," she hissed, but not quietly enough — the mapmaker glanced over at them. There was something hungry in his gaze. Then his lips set in a thin line.

"You should have listened to me, Beast Riders. Now you will pay the price!"

He lifted his hands to the edges of the hood, and Tanner noticed that ink no longer stained his fingers.

Instead, they had grown longer, with knobbled joints and sickly yellowing skin. His nails were sharp. And as he pulled back his hood, it wasn't Jonas who stood before them.

"Vendrake!" Tanner gasped. He'd disguised himself as the person closest to Gwen after her brother, just to get near to them and try to get the mask back.

Derthsin's servant grinned crookedly. The scar that snaked across his pale skin bloomed an angry red, and he threw off the cloak to reveal tight-fitting black leather armor.

"My master sends his regards," he said.

"Send him *this* back!" said Castor, drawing his sword. Gwen had moved a short distance away.

"I'd think very carefully before you do anything foolish," hissed Vendrake, his eyes darting from one to the other. "Jonas died a slow and painful death because he would not bow to Derthsin's will. Do not make the same mistake."

A shape appeared in the sky behind Vendrake, growing bigger as it approached. A vulture, almost as huge as Firepos, dragged a flying chariot by creaking harnesses. The bird's black eyes glittered in its bald,

45

mottled head. The matted feathers of its wings had been torn away in places, leaving bare, wrinkled flesh.

There was a hissing sound and the vulture had to jerk clumsily to one side as an ax sliced through the air. A small distance away from Tanner, Gwen was already reaching for another ax from her belt, sending it arcing toward the bird. There was a squawk of pain and blood spattered down toward them. Even from this distance, Tanner could see the red streaks staining the vulture's feathers.

"You'll pay for that, little girl!" shouted Vendrake. He lunged toward her, but Tanner drew his sword and leaped between them, the point of his weapon trained on Vendrake's heart. Derthsin's servant hesitated before stalking off toward the chariot. They watched him leave, but Tanner knew things were only going to get worse.

"He came here for a reason," he said as Gwen and Castor drew near. Rufus was staring after the vulture, his fingers twitching as he murmured to himself. "Rufus! Is there anything you can do?" Tanner demanded.

The vulture had landed on the ground. Vendrake was smoothing a hand over the bird's wounds and the evil bird ruffled its feathers, visibly improved. What evil magic had Vendrake used to cure the vulture?

"Rufus!" Tanner called again, his patience running out. Their friend took a deep breath and sent bolts of light shooting out from his fingers toward where the vulture had landed. Instantly, the chariot caught alight, flames flickering around the edges of the varnished wood. Vendrake glanced back at them, snarling. He used his cloak to pat out the flames before leaping into the chariot through clouds of smoke. His curses carried through the air toward them.

"You don't understand what you're dealing with!" he shouted.

"This isn't working," Tanner cried. "We're just making him more angry."

"I can finish him," Castor said, his hand going to his sword as he marched forward. But even as he spoke, the vulture heaved the chariot into the air with Vendrake in it. It circled once, then descended sharply toward them. Tanner and Castor leaped aside, but it was only as Tanner rolled behind a rock that he heard Gwen's scream.

"No!" Tanner ran out from behind the boulder, but it was too late. Gwen's legs dangled in the air as the vulture held her arm in its beak, then — with a vicious swing of its head — threw her into the chariot. Vendrake laughed loudly.

"The game is on!" he called down. Tanner could hear the blood pumping in his ears, his heart almost bursting through his chest as fury tore through him.

Channel it, came Firepos's wise words. *Don't lose control of your anger. Use it to get Gwen back.*

Derthsin's minion had already stolen Geffen away once, dragging him through the Avantian skies to General Gor. Was he going to do the same to Gwen? But even as these thoughts swirled around Tanner's head, the chariot lunged down between the trees, heading toward something hidden. *What have they spotted?*

Tanner leaped from boulder to boulder and darted into the forest.

"Wait for us!" called Castor.

Tanner heard his friends crashing through the forest behind him but didn't stop. A harsh squawk tore the air as the vulture-drawn chariot emerged from the trees, sailing overhead. Vendrake was laughing now, and Gwen clung to the edge of the chariot, blood scoring her arm from where the vulture had grabbed her.

Tanner stumbled over a tree root and sprawled headlong onto the mossy ground. Picking himself up, he heard a terrifying sound: Gulkien yowling in pain.

"Help!" screamed Gwen from the chariot. "Gulkien!"

Tanner emerged into a clearing and his blood froze in his veins. Gulkien lay on his side with a deep gouge matting his gray fur with blood. He tried to stand and sagged back down.

The vulture swooped through the air, its talons reaching for Rufus next. Tanner pushed the other boy aside and threw himself at the chariot as it rose above him, catching the rim of one wheel from below. His arms were almost ripped from their sockets as the vulture jerked higher on its ragged wings. The trees fell away beneath them.

"Get off me!" he heard Gwen say.

"You're Derthsin's now!" shouted Vendrake. Tanner heard a heavy thump and Gwen groaned.

The vulture wheeled in the air, and wind blasted through Tanner's clothes. He saw Firepos's blazing wings spread below as the Beast took off in pursuit.

I'm coming, she called to Tanner.

Beneath her, Castor and Rufus darted between the trees, their eyes fixed on the sky. Nera and Falkor stayed close to their sides, but Tanner realized there was little the Beasts could do.

It's up to me now, he thought.

The air turned icy, and Tanner could hardly feel his fingers. Gritting his teeth, he pulled himself up and reached for the edge of the chariot. He heaved his body over it and tumbled inside.

"What's this?" shouted Vendrake. "Another passenger! My master will be pleased."

Tanner gripped the side of the chariot to steady himself and faced Derthsin's servant. The chariot tipped dangerously to one side, almost unfooting Tanner. Vendrake stood perfectly balanced, and behind his legs Gwen lay passed out on the floor, her cloak fallen back to reveal her throwing axes. Blood streaked her arm. Tanner's stomach curled into a ball of fury.

"You'll regret letting your vulture hurt her!" he said, as he drew his sword.

"My vulture and I do as my master wishes," Vendrake replied.

There was a screeching sound as a panel in the floor of the chariot slid open. Tanner glanced down to see snakes writhing out of a hidden compartment, their fangs bared. He leaped to one side, but already the cold scales of a vicious-looking viper curled around his ankle. He leaned against the side of the chariot and tried to kick it off, but the coils only tightened. More snakes were moving over the prone body of Gwen, and Vendrake sat at the helm of the chariot with his arms folded, laughing.

"There's nothing you can do," goaded Derthsin's servant, the scar on his jaw puckering around his crooked smile. "Either you go over the side and plunge to your death, or you stay here and have the life squeezed out of you. What's it to be?"

Tanner didn't answer. Instead, he began hacking madly at the snakes around him. Lengths of muscular flesh sent blood spurting as he cut heads from bodies, bringing his blade dangerously near his own limbs as he freed himself. A final slice of the sword and the viper around his ankles fell to the floor, the white of its spine chillingly stark against the stain of blood on its scales.

Tanner threw himself toward Gwen and tore at the snakes writhing over her, flinging them out of the chariot. One of the snakes opened its mouth wide, pulling its head back, fangs ready to fill his veins with poison. Tanner brought his sword around in a low arc and cut the snake in two so that the pieces of its body fell beside his knees.

Vendrake had stopped laughing.

"You have a surprising power," he murmured, watching Tanner closely. "It's true what they say. A Beast's blood really does bring strength." *So Vendrake knows,* Tanner thought.

A screech pierced Tanner's ears. Firepos was catching up to them with strong wing beats, flames licking over her feathers. Vendrake laughed.

"Your Beast is useless," he said. "She can't attack without killing you, too."

Tanner knew he was right. If Firepos used one of her fireballs, the whole chariot would be burned to ashes. But as it wobbled, setting the harnesses clanking and the snakes slithering across the floor, another idea flashed in his mind.

He sent a message to Firepos: *Fly below the chariot, quickly.*

The freezing gale whipped around Tanner and snatched at Vendrake's dark cloak. As it did so, Tanner glimpsed the hideous scar covering Vendrake's flesh. It spread across the lower part of his jaw and trailed in shining ridges down onto his neck, where it disappeared beneath the leather tunic.

"Admiring my beauty, are you?" snarled his foe.

"It's no less than you deserve," snapped Tanner.

He'd discovered that Vendrake had been captured and tortured by Derthsin long ago; now he was his faithful servant, bound to the evil that his master spread.

Vendrake sneered bitterly and reached inside the cloak to his hip. The snakes slipped back into the hidden cavity in the floor of the chariot and the panel clicked into place above them. What was happening now? Tanner's grip tightened on his sword hilt as his enemy drew out a wooden baton connected to several snaking lengths of knotted leather. A cat-o'-nine-tails.

Vendrake gave him a smile. "If the snakes don't work against you, then the cat will have to." He gazed at the dangling thongs. "When he'd finished with me, Derthsin left this by my side — in a pool of my own blood." He began to swirl the handle, spinning the knotted cords, and spoke in a low, lilting chant:

> *A knotted rope around your neck*
> *Is all it takes to kill,*
> *Derthsin's wish is spelled in blood*
> *For his servants to fulfill."*

The notes cut through the air like ice. Grandmother Esme had sung Tanner a lullaby to the same tune when he was a young boy.

Vendrake smiled, and the vulture turned its scraggy neck, letting out an excited squawk. Its eyes glittered with greed.

"She knows it's time for a meal," said Vendrake.

He lashed with the cat-o'-nine-tails, and Tanner ducked as the thongs cracked above his head. He searched desperately for Firepos but couldn't see her. *Where are you?*

"I'll cut you to ribbons!" roared Vendrake. Gwen let out a moan.

Tanner spun around and dove, slamming into the other side of the chariot. The knotted leather swished past his shoulder and snapped across the chariot wall, tearing out splinters of wood. He crouched in the enclosed space and lunged with his sword, but Vendrake skipped nimbly out of the way, dragging the thongs across Tanner's forearm. The contact was only light, but a stinging pain made Tanner gasp. Beads of blood smeared his arm. The thongs wrapped around his sword, and Vendrake yanked on the handle of his whip. Tanner couldn't hold on as the hilt was pulled from his hand. His only weapon spiraled over the edge of the chariot.

The vulture screeched with triumph.

"My creature can have your flesh," said Vendrake. "I'll save your skin to hang from Derthsin's chamber wall."

A voice intruded on Tanner's thoughts: *I'm here.*

Firepos! His Beast was in place.

Tanner grinned at Vendrake. "Come and get me, then!"

As his enemy stepped forward again, raising the snaking thongs, there was a blur of movement and Vendrake suddenly tripped onto his face with a grunt of surprise. A hand gripped his ankle — Gwen's! She let go, her face twisted in a grimace as she looked at her palm. It was coated in green slime and mold that had come off Vendrake's leg.

Just like Geffen's skin, thought Tanner. *Of course!* No one could survive the wounds that Derthsin had inflicted on Vendrake. . . .

Gwen's woozy gaze met his.

"Vendrake's a corpse!" Tanner shouted to her.

Vendrake scrambled to his feet, his lip curled into a sneer. "None live to breathe after Derthsin's rage," he said. He kicked Tanner hard in the stomach, sending him reeling against the back of the chariot. Through his pain, Tanner saw Vendrake turn on Gwen and lift the whip over her head. "You'll soon see for yourselves."

Here we go, Tanner told Firepos.

He threw himself against the edge of the chariot. It tipped, making Vendrake stumble and desperately grip the side. As the world turned upside down and his stomach climbed into his throat, Tanner felt himself fall.

CHAPTER 4

Tanner tumbled through the air, catching flashes of Gwen's rolling body. He slammed into something soft and warm — Firepos's waiting back. His hands closed on her feathers. Gwen bounced off a wing and plummeted toward the ground.

"Gwen!"

Tanner scrambled up to Firepos's neck, his heart racing, and looked down. Gwen was lying face-first over Gulkien's broad, gray-haired back. *He's come to the rescue, too!*

The wolf howled as his leathery wings rose and fell. His flank was still bleeding, but not heavily. Gwen sat up groggily, her face pale and arm bruised. She threw a leg over his ridged spine, then looked up to Tanner and nodded in gratitude.

58

Tanner noticed his sword clutched in Firepos's talons. He stroked the flame bird's neck. "You saved our lives!" he said.

Weak flames rippled along her wings as she banked down and right, her golden beak glinting in a ray of sun. Tanner could see from her trembling wing tips that she was struggling to stay aloft. The bruised Avantian landscape slipped below them, and Tanner's heart clouded. *She's tired,* he realized. But her weariness seemed to run deeper than the exhaustion they were all feeling. *Is it because I drank her blood?* he thought.

He remembered Hilda, the old woman at Hartwell, passing him the vial that contained the thick liquid. She'd said she bought it from a traveler. . . .

Vendrake, disguised as Jonas.

Dread seeped through Tanner. Derthsin's minion must have used Firepos's blood to subvert Tanner's mission. Now, the bravery and strength of a Beast flowed through his veins, but at a cost to Firepos, making her weak. He stroked her golden feathers. He'd been a fool to drink it. He'd played into Derthsin's hands and betrayed Firepos. Derthsin must have guessed that Tanner would be tempted to wear a piece of the mask, that the strength from Firepos could be twisted into hate-filled bloodlust. *Derthsin gambled and won*, Tanner thought bitterly. *Firepos is weak and getting weaker, and battles fill me with a fury I can hardly control.*

"I'm sorry," he murmured.

You couldn't have known, came the message back. *You're a brave warrior now, fighting to save Avantia.* That much was true, Tanner knew. He still wanted to save his kingdom. All of this had to be worth something, didn't it? He'd set out on this journey to avenge Esme's death, but somewhere along the way it had become bigger than that — about saving Avantia from Derthsin's evil. He still wanted that, and he'd still fight for it.

Tanner glanced up as Vendrake's Beast dipped after them.

"Coward," Tanner yelled at Vendrake, "creeping around in disguise!"

Vendrake gripped both reins and steered the vulture in a low swoop past the Beasts.

"I've watched all of you," he sneered. "Ask Castor why he wasn't in the mines near his village!"

The words flew like a weapon through the air. Then Vendrake whipped the reins and the vulture climbed again.

"The mines?" Tanner muttered to himself.

He watched the chariot disappear to the west, heading for the volcano. *And for Derthsin,* thought Tanner grimly. *His master will soon know we're coming.* Why had he allowed Gwen to believe that man was Jonas? Hadn't they learned anything by now? *No one is to be trusted,* Tanner thought. *Not even the faces of the people we love.*

Firepos spread her wings and landed beside Gulkien, back at the entrance to their cave. The wolf growled a greeting. Gwen inspected her Beast's wound with an anxious face; it was nearly healed, thanks to the Beasts' ability to cure themselves. She barely seemed to notice the dried blood on her own arm. As Tanner slipped off Firepos, Castor came to his side and gave him a punch on the shoulder.

"That was some stunt!" He grinned. "Did you *know* the Beasts were right below?"

Tanner knew that Castor was trying to lighten the mood, but his stomach felt tight with nerves. Their pursuit of the last piece of the mask was already going wrong. Tanner had no right to call himself a hero, or even a survivor. It seemed as though he was failing at everything he did.

Rufus stood at a distance, watching them carefully. When he saw Tanner's glance, he approached.

"You could have died," he said, his lips white with anxiety. Falkor hissed slowly and blinked his polished black eyes. "He's pleased you're safe." Rufus nodded to Gulkien. "Come here, Gwen. Let me see your injury."

Gwen did as he asked, lifting her arm. The skin was tight and swollen around deep scratches and trails of dried blood.

Rufus turned her arm over so that he could take a closer look, then pointed with his staff, muttering a few strange-sounding words. Blue smoke stretched in tendrils from the staff's tip and settled over the scratches like a cloud. Gulkien snarled and licked his fangs, watching his mistress. But as the mist cleared, the skin on her arm had healed over.

"That's amazing!" said Gwen, gazing at the unblemished pink skin.

Rufus flushed. "It's the least I can do," he said with a shrug.

Castor started to walk over to Nera. "Come on, we've wasted enough time."

"Wait a minute," said Tanner, remembering Vendrake's odd parting words. "I need to ask you something. About the mines."

Gwen raised her eyebrows.

"Can't it wait?" asked Castor, looking away. "Derthsin's probably found the final piece of the mask by now! And then he'll be after us for the other pieces. Our lives are in danger, for Avantia's sake!" His face was flushed with emotion.

Tanner folded his arms. "Well, let's make it quick. How come you weren't trapped down there, too? Captain Brutus took all the other men and boys from Colton, but not you."

Tread carefully, Firepos warned him. *A friend's heart is not to be torn out.*

But he ignored his Beast. Tanner realized these

questions had always been playing around the edges of his mind. Why had it taken Vendrake's sinister prompting to make him say the words out loud?

Castor shrugged, but still his eyes were downcast. He drew his sword and looked along the blade, making a show of inspecting it. "How should I know?"

Gwen put her hand on his arm. "Come on, Castor, you can tell us. If I were Brutus, I'd have picked you out. You must have been the strongest boy in the village with those muscles of yours."

A faint smiled flashed over Castor's face, but it quickly fell away. He sighed.

"Just tell us," Gwen said softly. "Or would you rather we heard the reason from Vendrake, or Derthsin himself?"

Castor took a deep breath and stared off over the trees. "I made a deal," he said, his voice barely a whisper. Finally, he looked at them, his eyes full of despair. "I didn't know they were bad at first."

"Who?" asked Tanner.

"Gor and his men. He said he was raising an army. Well paid. To protect the kingdom. He wanted lists of all the men in the village. He said he'd make me a sergeant."

Rufus was the first to speak. "So you handed them over," he said.

"I didn't realize until it was too late," said Castor. He was slicing through the air with his sword now, cutting figure eights. His movements became quicker and more clumsy as he continued to speak. He looked away from them. "Gor turned nasty and sent his men to drag everyone from their houses. He said they'd work in the mines until they fell to the ground dead."

"And you did nothing to stop this?" said Rufus, throwing down his staff in disgust.

"Rufus . . ." Gwen began.

"What could I do?" asked Castor, his blade gleaming. He took a menacing step toward Rufus, who backed away. "Gor said he'd kill all the women and children if I didn't help. He told me he needed a contact in Colton. Someone to tell him if anyone suspicious showed up."

"A spy *and* a coward," said Rufus.

Tanner half expected Castor to hold his sword to

Rufus's throat, but instead his shoulders slumped and he sheathed the blade.

"That's right," he whispered, almost to himself. "A coward."

"But you didn't hand me and Tanner over," Gwen interrupted. "You fought with us to free the people of your village. You helped save my brother!"

"He bought his own freedom by selling his people into slavery!" shouted Rufus.

"Yes, and he also saved your sister — or have you forgotten that?" Gwen gasped.

Rufus ignored her, his face coloring. "I should've stayed in my cave!" Falkor stirred his shimmering scales and hissed angrily in agreement.

"Well, tough. You didn't, did you? You came with us," said Gwen. "We need to pull together now."

But anger rose up in Tanner's chest, as unstoppable as a geyser. He was remembering all the times Castor had taunted him. Always pretending to be so brave, so undaunted. Always putting everyone else down to make himself look better.

"Rufus is right," he said. "We don't need cowards."

As the words left his mouth, Gwen gaped at him in astonishment. Firepos fluttered her wing tips. She was trying to communicate, but Tanner shut off his mind to her. He wouldn't be told what to do!

Even as he looked at Castor, he could see he was spoiling for a fight. And Tanner wanted to fight. Heat spread over his skin, his veins throbbing. His eyes sought out Rufus, boring into the young wizard's cloak. The pieces of the mask were calling to him, begging him to put them on his face again, to feel the sparks in his blood, the surging power. . . .

"Are you all right?" asked Gwen.

Her voice snapped him to attention, and his body cooled.

Castor looked stiffly from one face to the next. "I'm glad you're safe, Gwen," he said thickly. He turned to Tanner. "You've always hated me, haven't you? Well, I never meant to hurt anybody. Remember that."

Castor stepped up on a boulder and leaped nimbly onto Nera's back. His Beast scraped the rocks with her claws and roared, taking a step away.

"Don't go!" shouted Gwen. She rushed forward, but Rufus gripped her arm.

With a lash of her tail, Nera sprang down the slope and into the forest.

"Good riddance to them, I say," said Rufus.

The fury seeped from Tanner's blood, and he felt shame. He looked to Firepos, who stared at him with reproach. *What have I done?* he asked silently.

Gwen threw off Rufus's arm and leaned against Gulkien, her face buried in his fur.

A gentle breeze ruffled Firepos's feathers and her reply sent a chill across Tanner's skin. *You pushed him away.*

CHAPTER 5

*N*era has gone. She takes her Chosen Rider with her, and our fate is more uncertain than ever. The group of four is broken.

The ancient fire sweeps over me, consuming my bones in pain. There's no escaping the curse of the flame bird, as foretold by Anoret. Her words come back to me again:

> The bravery in Beasts' blood
> Shall set fire to the final fight,
> The curse of the phoenix
> Shall make a companion falter
> But Justice will find the Mighty.

I don't understand all of Anoret's predictions, but I know that the future approaches as surely as the sun will *rise and set. Falkor slithers closer, the slits of his eyes gleaming with concern. His tongue flickers, sensing my pain. Gulkien pads toward me and rubs his muzzle into my feathers.* It's all right, my fellow Beasts, I have long guessed where my destiny lies.

I turn toward the west. It's time to return, my friends. Time to make our way to my birthplace. The volcano calls to me, and I am powerless to resist.

"What's wrong with them?" asked Rufus.

Tanner watched the Beasts gather together with a sense of dread. Firepos's eyes blazed and her talons clawed at the rock. He'd never seen her so agitated, and the waves of her anxiety crashed into him.

She wants us to leave, he realized. They'd called after Castor for hours with no luck, searching the surrounding fields and forests. But he was gone for good. Eventually, they'd camped out for the night, waking cold and with stiff joints.

"We have to go to the volcano — right now," Tanner said, climbing to his feet and stretching his limbs.

"But with only three of us to face Derthsin —" Gwen began.

"The last piece of the mask is too important," Tanner interrupted. "We're strong enough. We have to be."

Did he really believe that, though? Despite his arrogance, Castor's sword skills were second to none, and without him they were seriously weakened as a force.

Gulkien's growl drew everyone's attention. Falkor hissed aggressively and slithered to Rufus's side. Firepos flapped her wings, bathing them all in the warmth of her inner fire. She screeched, and the sound echoed around them, filling Tanner's heart with pride.

"It looks like the Beasts agree with me," said Tanner. "We have to go."

He scrambled up Firepos's feathers and settled across her back. Her sharp beak pointed directly toward the morning sun in the east, as if she could see their destination already.

Falkor writhed at Firepos's side as Rufus laid his staff across his dark scales. She lifted her head and hissed back toward Gulkien, who tested his wings with huge drafts of air.

"I don't think we need to check the map again," said Gwen. "The Beasts seem to know where they're going."

As Firepos took to the skies, the wind seeping through Tanner's clothes, Falkor set off, sliding across the ground in pulsing waves. Gulkien's tongue lolled from his jaws as he flew headlong beside them. Tanner looked back. *It doesn't feel right with only three of us,* he thought.

They flew directly into the warm glow of the sun's rays. Tanner squinted at the horizon ahead, feeling dread grip his insides. Since the morning he'd buried his grandmother beside their cottage, he'd known that he'd have to face the full might of Derthsin's army one day. Maybe he'd known even on the dark day the evil lord killed his father and dragged his mother away. He'd been too young to fight back then.

"But I'm coming for you now, Derthsin," Tanner promised. They were headed toward the volcano, where the fourth piece of the mask was. Perhaps

Derthsin was already there. *So be it*, Tanner thought. It was time to end this.

They flew over what seemed like endless plains. Here and there were the ruins of villages, charred buildings, abandoned fields, and the rotting carcasses of slaughtered cattle. They passed over the ominous mounds of hastily dug graves. People seemed to have abandoned their ruined homes, or else they cowered indoors, terrified to come out. It was as if Derthsin had poisoned the whole kingdom with his evil.

Tanner watched the horizon for any sign of enemy soldiers, and scanned the sky until his eyes hurt in case Vendrake reappeared in his dreadful, vulture-drawn chariot. The morning had given way to dark clouds that blotted out the sun completely and seemed to press heavily on the scourged landscape.

Firepos suddenly twisted her head downward and dove, with Gulkien copying the maneuver.

"What's happening?" Gwen shouted across.

"I don't know," Tanner replied.

Falkor had stopped, and lay with his head a hands-breadth from the ground, his forked tongue darting in and out. Firepos and Gulkien swooped alongside him, hovering a few paces off the ground.

"My Beast senses something ahead," Rufus said. "Let's be careful."

"I wonder if it's Castor," said Gwen hopefully.

Firepos gained height again with powerful wing strokes, and they flew low with Falkor slightly ahead, tasting the air for danger. As they broke over the top of a low rise, Tanner gasped.

A crowd of hundreds seethed over the plain in a solid mass. The thunder of their combined footsteps seemed to shake the air.

"It's an army!" said Gwen.

Tanner's stomach lurched with fear. He tugged on Firepos's feathers to guide her higher, and the Beast responded by striking upward with powerful beats of her wings. They rose over the troops, but as he looked down, Tanner realized these couldn't be Derthsin's men. They marched without order and wore no armor, and they had none of the vicious varkules among their cavalry. Instead he saw men and women of all ages, some on horses, most on foot. Many of them carried makeshift weapons — pieces of plows, woodcutters' axes, shepherd's crooks, and threshers from the fields. Some carried bows and arrows. Real weapons glinted in the hands of a few, but they looked clean and unused. A handful had shields, but most walked without protection in simple tunics, or at most breastplates made of toughened leather.

They must be from all the ransacked villages, Tanner thought. *But are they friends or enemies?* Derthsin had wrung the goodness from Geffen's soul — he could have done the same to these people.

As they glided overhead, faces turned upward one by one, and the mass of peasant folk ground to a halt. Tanner heard shouts of fear.

"Land ahead of them," he called across to Gwen. "Not too close, just in case."

He steered Firepos in a wide loop and approached the front of the marchers. The flame bird tipped her wings to slow her descent, and alighted on the grassy plains. A moment later Gulkien bounded beside them, folding his leathered wings into his fur.

"Stay back here," Tanner said, slipping off Firepos's back.

"Are you sure that's wise?" asked Gwen.

"I don't want to scare them," said Tanner. "If they're the enemy, then we'll know soon enough."

Keeping his hand on the hilt of his sword, Tanner walked confidently toward the leaders, a line of rugged-looking men. Gwen, he noticed, had hooked her hands into her belt, near her throwing axes. *But if there's trouble, we won't stand a chance. There's too many of them.*

Low muttering passed through the armed band, and Tanner felt hundreds of eyes fixing him with hatred. He was about to lift his hand in greeting when he heard the *twang* of a bowstring. An arrow thudded into the ground at his feet.

"Take another step, and it will be your last," said a woman's voice. Tanner spied the archer stringing another shaft.

"Fire that arrow, and you'll lose your arm," shouted Gwen, running to Tanner's side. She had a throwing ax lifted above her shoulder.

Tanner swallowed.

"Kill them!" someone shouted. "They're Derthsin's servants!"

Relief flooded through Tanner. They were on the same side.

The woman's arms twitched as she pulled the bow-string tighter.

"We're not your enemy!" Tanner shouted.

"He's lying," someone yelled back from among the ranks. "Why else do they have Beasts?"

"Put down your ax," Tanner said to Gwen, loud enough that the front rows of the army could hear.

"Are you crazy?" she hissed.

"Do it," he said. "We need to show we're not a threat."

Tanner dropped his hand to his belt. Slowly, he unclipped his sheath and let his sword fall to the ground. Beside him, Gwen cast her ax behind her.

"See!" he shouted. "We mean you no harm."

A stout man stood at the center of the party, wearing a scarlet cloak. He had steel-gray hair, knotted hands, and the weather-beaten skin of a farmer. "My name is Affren. Do you swear that you and your . . . your friends come in peace?"

"We ride our Beasts against the forces of Derthsin," said Tanner, holding out his hand.

There was a disturbance in the crowd, and then a girl burst out. She ran toward Rufus, laughing joyously.

"Isadora!" Rufus cried. He jumped off Falkor's back and embraced his sister. "You're safe! What happened to you?"

"I bought a horse and rode to Colweir, like you said I should," she said. "I told the people there what you were doing, and how you saved me. We talked of the evil invaders, and we decided to gather our weapons and march out to fight!"

Rufus looked at his sister with love and admiration. "You started this army?" he asked.

"I did, and we are all willing to fight with you against Derthsin!"

Tanner remembered the terrified little girl they had rescued from the followers of Derthsin a few days earlier. She had changed a lot in that time.

A murmur passed through the crowd as they saw this happy reunion. "Lower your bow, Breda," Affren said.

The archer did as she was ordered, and Affren stepped forward, taking Tanner's hand. "You are so young, yet you set yourself against Derthsin? His armies have ravaged our kingdom."

Tanner nodded. "We know. We've already fought some of Derthsin's armies. And we have four — I mean — three Beasts to help us." He didn't dare glance at Gwen; he knew how crestfallen she'd look.

Though Affren carried only a staff sharpened to a point and blackened in the fire, the man beside him had a finely turned shield, covered in tough leather and embossed with iron points.

"Some of your weapons are well-crafted," said Tanner. "Do you have trained soldiers, too?"

"What weapons we have are from the caves in the northern mountains," said Affren.

"Derthsin's armory!" said Gwen.

"You know of the place?" asked Affren, as his comrades muttered.

"We destroyed it," said Tanner. "With the help of our friends."

A young man stepped to Affren's side, carrying a large, double-edged blade with a wide hilt. "I knew it was true," he said. "Many of the men have talked of four heroes, told stories about the 'Justice of the Mighty.' I just didn't realize the heroes would be so young."

"We've seen our share of death and battle," Tanner retorted. The words the young man had used reminded him of the prophecy Firepos had shared. Where had he heard those stories?

"Forgive Raurk," said Affren, nodding at the younger man. "We live in uncertain times." He looked past Tanner, to where Firepos and Gulkien waited. "Where is your fourth comrade?"

Tanner glanced at Gwen. It would do Affren and his army no good to know the desperate truth. "He's lost," he said.

"Whether you be four, or three, or fifty," said Affren, "I fear the kingdom is lost already."

He gazed sadly at Tanner, his watery eyes filled with a grief that couldn't be put into words.

Tanner's head swam as he remembered Esme and the mission she'd sent him on. He felt suddenly light and his knees weak to the point of buckling. After all he'd been through, carried by anger and sheer luck, the final task seemed just too daunting. Each time they'd faced Gor, he'd survived, but they'd lost something. Esme, Geffen, and now Castor was gone, too. And still Derthsin awaited.

Affren's eyes hadn't left him.

This man must have lived four times as long as me, Tanner thought. *What can I tell him?*

That it isn't numbers or weapons that will save this kingdom, came Firepos's voice, *but courage and the will to survive. You can be what they need — a leader.*

The Beast's words lit a spark in Tanner's chest. Derthsin's army moved quickly across the land, crushing villages beneath its iron fist before the people had the chance to gather and defend themselves. This ragtag army of survivors had lost everything — their homes, livelihoods, and relatives. He didn't know if they could fight, or how their makeshift weapons would stand up to the cold steel of Derthsin's forces. He couldn't tell if they would hold firm in front of a varkule's drooling jaws and blaring war horns. But in their eyes burned sorrow and anger. If he could harness those feelings, and find a way to direct them, perhaps . . .

"We can fight together," he said aloud.

Raurk laughed bitterly, and swept his arm in a wide gesture toward the massed villagers. "We don't march to fight," he said. "We stick together for safety, to forage for food."

"Join us," said Tanner. The flame of hope seemed to grow in his chest. If people were gathering like this, daring to show themselves openly with weapons, it meant he and his companions weren't the only people fighting Derthsin. Others in Avantia were rebelling, too! "Together we might be strong enough to take on our common enemy."

"And if not?" said Raurk. "Should we die for nothing? At least if we don't oppose Derthsin, he might let us live."

"He may let you keep your lives," Gwen cut in. "But at the cost of your freedom."

"And how long will it be before Derthsin's mercy snaps?" said Tanner. "We've seen the ruins of this kingdom. We *know* how little Derthsin cares for the people of Avantia."

Affren and Raurk shared a glance. "You say you have seen combat already," said Affren. "You've faced the varkules?"

Tanner nodded. "We have faced them and killed them," he said.

"One of those creatures tore my brother apart," said Raurk.

"Their Horse Beast trampled my wife," Affren added, his voice cracked with anger and grief.

"Derthsin's soldiers are wicked and cruel, but they are only people like you," said Gwen. "They *can* be beaten."

Tanner thought he saw the older man give a small nod, but Raurk still looked unsure. If he couldn't win them over with persuasion, perhaps he needed to try something else. "See this red cloth?" he said, raising his wrist. "It belonged to someone dear to me. My grandmother. Derthsin's army killed her without a thought. I fight for her. Fight for your wife, your brother — all those you have lost."

Raurk's expression hardened. "You're right," he said. "We can't live our lives in fear."

A few of those standing nearby mumbled their agreement, and pride flickered in Tanner's chest. He addressed Affren. "So you'll march with us against Derthsin? We're heading toward the volcano near my village. I can guarantee his men will be waiting for us there." With the location of the mask marked on their map, Tanner knew that their enemies would be headed toward it, too. Geffen had seen the map and would have shared all its secrets with General Gor.

The old man nodded firmly. "What do we have to lose?"

Tanner grinned. As he strapped his sword back around his waist, Gwen placed a hand on his shoulder. "With so many, we might just be able to get the final piece of the mask."

Tanner looked at his friend grimly. "For all our sakes, I hope so."

CHAPTER 6

The evening sun seemed to bring no warmth, and it bathed the plains in a red glow the color of washed-out bloodstains. Tanner flew over the troops, pointing to direct the foot soldiers into position. After his battles with General Gor, he had a better idea of how to arrange his new recruits. *Only weeks ago I was a baker's assistant, loading loaves into the oven. Now I'm directing men, possibly to their deaths.* But this was what he felt born to do. All those training sessions with Firepos as a young boy — they made sense now.

Affren sat behind him, clutching his waist, his scarlet cape billowing. "Do you ever get used to this?" he shouted over the breeze.

"Eventually!" replied Tanner cheerfully, trying to disguise the fear in the pit of his stomach. He wanted the rebel leader to see things from the air, though it had taken a little coaxing to get him to climb Firepos's feathers. So far they'd placed the baggage and weapons carts in the center of the force, protected by two columns of infantry, four deep, at either side. The cavalry, a hundred horsemen or so, were lined up at the front.

"They're your shock troops," said Tanner. "They can attack and wheel back quickly. Or, if they're successful, they can push forward through the enemy lines and attack them from the rear."

He pointed to the two ranks of archers stationed at the rear.

"The bowmen will be safe back there," said Tanner, "so they can focus on sending a steady barrage of arrows over the infantry." The words of war spilled easily from him.

"How do you know all this?" asked Affren.

"I've watched Derthsin's forces in action," said Tanner.

He'd seen plenty of battles since Derthsin's soldiers began their deadly march across the kingdom. In each one — at Forton, at Colton, and by the Southern

Caves — he remembered how the enemy had attacked. But there was a big difference between planning tactics from the air and fighting in the heat of battle. Would this army of amateurs really hold their shape when they faced the marauding enemy and fear froze their limbs?

A message floated up from Firepos: *Time will tell*.

Progress across the plains was slower with the hundreds of men below. Normally, Tanner and Firepos could have swooped over the terrain, but they couldn't afford to leave the army behind, so they zigzagged back and forth, trying to keep it in formation.

Rufus on Falkor scouted ahead while Gwen flew alongside Tanner.

"They look good," she said. "Castor would be in his element here."

Her words left Tanner feeling hollow. Occasionally he saw a shadow out of the corner of his eye and expected to see Nera leaping across the plain, but the magnificent Beast and her rider never appeared.

"I'm so pleased that Rufus and Isadora are together again," Gwen said. "Something good has happened at last."

Tanner nodded, deep in thought. "We should rest when we find water," he said.

As the smell of roasting meat and fish spread across the camp, Firepos hovered above Tanner. She cawed to him softly. "What is it?" he asked.

Look, came her voice.

Tanner searched out the Looking Crystal and held it to his eye. The milky stone swirled and cleared, so that distant objects leaped forward. At first Tanner saw nothing but the glinting pricks of stars in the dark blue of the night sky, but then a flash of red came into view. He twisted the Crystal into focus and made out the black silhouette of the volcano. An explosion of molten rock seemed to spout in slow motion, cascading down the black slopes.

"Why's it erupting now?" Tanner muttered.

"What can you see?" asked Rufus. Tanner lowered the Crystal and saw the wizard and Gwen beside him.

Rufus held a bowl of steaming stew, while Gwen passed Tanner a leg of rabbit.

"Look for yourself," said Tanner, handing over the Crystal. Rufus took it and turned toward the distant horizon. Even without the Looking Crystal, Tanner could see the faint orange glow.

"I've had a bad feeling since we stopped," said Rufus. "Evil lurks there. Magic stronger than anything I've felt before."

One of the logs in the campfire shifted, releasing a spiral of smoke. Tanner's breath caught in his throat as it wound into the shape of a figure, looming from the flames. Its pale face was unmistakable — those thin lips and the heavy brow.

"Derthsin!" said Tanner.

"What is it?" asked Gwen sharply. "What's the matter, Tanner?"

He turned to his friend. Her eyes were wide with concern.

"Can't you *see* that?" he said, pointing to the fire.

"See what?" she asked. "Tanner, you're scaring me."

Derthsin's voice sounded like whispering ashes. *"You have tasted power, young Beast Rider."*

89

Tanner stared into the flames, where the image lurked like a shadow. "What do you want?" he asked.

"We want the same thing," hissed the specter. "We want the mask."

"No," said Tanner. "I want to destroy it."

"What's the matter with him?" he heard Rufus say. "Who's he talking to?"

"I'm waiting for you," said Derthsin. Then he sent out a laugh like a death rattle.

The image collapsed back into the campfire. Tanner shivered, despite the fireside heat.

"I saw him," he muttered to his friends.

"Derthsin?" asked Rufus. "Here?"

"What did he say?" asked Gwen.

"He said he wants the mask," Tanner replied.

"Well, we know that!" Rufus scoffed. "Some message!"

Something had stopped Tanner from relaying the full message, the part about how *he* wanted the mask, too. He glanced across at Rufus's cloak. *I don't want it*, he told himself. *I just want to keep it out of Derthsin's hands.*

Gwen placed a hand on his knee. "Don't worry," she said. "We're here for you."

Tanner looked into the fire again, wondering if he might just have imagined it. Firepos landed beside him. She closed her huge wings, sending a draft through the flames.

I saw it, too, she said. *You should sleep. Tomorrow brings us closer to our destiny.*

Tanner leaned back into her warm feathers and tried to empty his mind.

At last, my Chosen Rider finds rest, and I open my eyes wide. I will watch over him, as I have every day since he was born.

All our lives will be threatened before the sun falls tomorrow. Mine is no more special than another's. Tanner grows into a leader of men, but he knows that his strength was bought at the cost of my weakness, and he hates himself for it. Poor boy. Does he not know that I would give every drop of my being for his sake? My only regret is that wearing that piece of the mask has made Tanner's fight even more difficult. But he will get through, he will survive.

As for me, none can save me. This much I know. It is as it should be, foretold by Anoret and glimpsed by Tanner. I embrace my fate and Tanner must, too.

The makeshift army struck camp as the glimmer of dawn pushed back the dark cowl of night. Tanner gazed out across the horizon, wondering what the day ahead would hold. *By nightfall, there'll have been more death,* he thought, shuddering. He felt sure that when he'd worn the mask, he'd seen the death of a Beast, heard a heartbeat slowing. Would it be Firepos? Or one of the others? But he had no choice — he had to see this out to the end. "There are too many hopes pinned on this," he muttered. "I can't turn back now."

As he climbed onto Firepos's back, Affren rushed up to his side. In his hands was his scarlet cape, folded up.

"What's this?" asked Tanner.

"Please," said Affren. "Wear it."

"But . . ."

"You're our leader now," said the villager. "The army respects you."

Tanner took the cape in his hands. The cloth was coarse and heavy, and he threw it over his shoulders.

"Thank you," he said. "I hope I don't let you down."

"You couldn't do that now," said Affren. "You've given us something to believe in."

Tanner took to the air in front of the cavalry, Gulkien and Gwen beside him. The first of the sun's rays glinted over the horizon at their backs. They flew ahead and doubled back, scouting the lands ahead as the army followed.

Cool mists squatted over the ground to the west, obscuring most of the view. Firepos descended, emerging over the smoking ruins of a settlement. Houses crumbled, their doors broken from their hinges. The bloated corpses of dead livestock littered the abandoned streets.

"Only ghosts live here now," Tanner muttered as Firepos lifted away.

• • •

Late morning, the sky turned lead-gray and condensation seeped through Tanner's clothes, chilling him to the bone. They left the rolling landscape, and dropped down into a plain dotted with hundreds of tree stumps among the long grasses.

This was once a forest, Tanner realized.

Every so often, Firepos called softly to Gulkien, who growled back. From the ground Falkor would hiss. The sounds were hesitant and cautious. *They're making their own battle plans,* Tanner realized. The Beasts were fighting for their lives, too. If Derthsin got his hands on the mask, he could control them for his own evil ends.

The flame bird gave a low screech in response, and heat surged through her feathers. Tanner gripped his Beast tighter as an orange glow shone through the fog.

"We're close!" he shouted to Gwen. "Tell the others!"

She nodded and placed a hand on the back on Gulkien's furry neck. The Wolf Beast dipped his head and sank through the air with the wind buffeting his leathery wings. Tanner fixed his eyes on the volcano's peak as they broke through the last shreds of mist.

His gaze fell from the spurting lava, down the scorched track where it flowed through the steep, forested slopes. His heart almost stopped when he saw what awaited them.

CHAPTER 7

A massive fortress built of black stone squatted half-way down the slope, guarding access to the volcano. Battlements, carved out of the rock face, towered over a moat of boiling lava. But the edges of the stones were still rough-hewn and none of the wood had been treated properly. This place had been built in a rush. Is that why he had heard no mention of its existence?

A huge gateway drawbridge, taller than any building Tanner had ever seen, was drawn up. *How will we even get inside?* he wondered.

Tanner took out his Looking Crystal and held it to his eye. The milky surface cleared. Along the turreted walls, he picked out hundreds of soldiers clutching bows. They all wore gleaming chain mail and helmets with jutting spikes. Some gripped spears and deadly pikes in their gauntleted hands.

"Derthsin's prepared," Tanner muttered to himself, steering Firepos toward Gwen and Gulkien. His friend looked over with a pale face, and Tanner tossed her the Crystal so she could take a look.

"Why don't they attack? Have they not seen us?" she asked.

She had a point. *Something's not right about this*, Tanner thought.

Suddenly, a commotion of shouting rose up from the army below, human cries mixed with animal snorts. Firepos dropped quickly through the cloud with Gulkien close behind. A terrible sight met Tanner's eyes. A horse lay on its side, eyes rolling wildly, while its rider, a young woman, desperately tried to get close to its flailing body.

"Poor thing!" cried Gwen.

The rest of the army had come to a halt behind. Falkor slithered through the crowd, Rufus clutching his back. As Firepos extended her claws, preparing to land, Tanner noticed that the horse's leg was enclosed in a rusty iron trap, its metal jaws buried in the flesh.

"Don't land!" Tanner yelled to Gwen. "There are traps!"

But Gulkien bounded onto the ground, and Gwen yelped as her Beast's paw seemed to disappear. The mossy turf fell away, revealing a mesh of branches laid over a pit. The wolf staggered, his hindquarters falling into the trap, while his front paws scrabbled for purchase at the edge. With a growl and a heave of his wings, he managed to tug himself to safety.

"Thank goodness!" breathed Gwen, sagging with relief over her Beast's back.

Firepos hovered over the concealed hole, and Tanner saw sharpened stakes lining the bottom. If Gulkien had fallen, his body would have been pierced through and he would have been unable to heal himself.

"Please! Oh, please. Help my horse!" the female rider called.

Falkor nosed closer to the fallen stallion, which had started to move more weakly. Rufus called to the watching crowd: "I need two strong men to pull the trap away."

Raurk ran forward with another soldier, while the woman stroked her horse's head. "There, there," she said soothingly. "Try to stay calm."

The injured creature shuddered as the men pulled the trap's jagged edges open. The flesh of the horse's leg hung in ribbons, and Tanner could see the gleam of exposed bone. The horse tried to stand but slumped down with a neigh of distress.

"Now, move back, all of you," said Rufus. He pointed his serpent's crook at the horse.

"What's he doing?" asked the woman, stepping away.

A pale blue light burst from the end of the staff and shot into the wound. As a wisp of smoke cleared, the hundreds of spectators gasped at once and Tanner saw a smile spread across Rufus's face. The bloody injury was completely healed.

"Oh, thank you!" cried the woman, her arms wrapped around the horse's neck. "How did you do it?" she asked Rufus.

As the young wizard exchanged explanations with the people below, Tanner flew closer to Gwen.

"I'm stupid," he said. "I should have known Derthsin wouldn't make it easy for us."

"Don't be so hard on yourself," she replied. "No one's hurt now."

But Tanner wasn't prepared to risk any more lives. "We need to find another way to the fortress," he said. "Tell the army to stay here for the time being."

He left Gwen and Gulkien with the soldiers and flew upward to get a better view. The folds of the scarlet cape fluttered around him. "I should never have offered to lead them if I can't keep them safe," he muttered.

War isn't without casualties, Firepos replied. *Remember that.*

Tanner steered the flame bird left, to the north. As he did, the plain broke up into uneven ground, and then fell away in a wide gorge through which a river flowed over stones and between boulders. There was no track, but at least the ground was too rocky for traps to be hidden. High walls ran along both sides of the gorge, which would help keep the army hidden from Derthsin's scouts.

"Not perfect," said Tanner. "But it will have to do."

He took a last glance at the hulking black fortress and told Firepos to descend back to the army. Every fiber of his being warned him that this was a place of death, and that he should turn around and fly away. But his heart gave him strength. *The last piece of the mask is in there somewhere*, he thought.

The army was happy to leave the dangerous long grasses, but the going was difficult up through the rocky gorge. The soldiers broke into a single-file march. Tanner flew low below the ridgeline, staying out of sight, and Gwen and Rufus took turns to climb up and take a look with the Crystal toward the fortress. Each time they reported back that the rows of enemy soldiers hadn't moved. So far, they hadn't been spotted.

The river became a small stream as they made their way slowly up the gorge. It took half a day before they reached the valley head, and at the summit, Firepos and Gulkien landed on a heap of boulders. Falkor wound between them and formed himself into a coil. Rufus was staring ahead, openmouthed.

Tanner climbed off Firepos's back and gazed across the remaining distance to the fortress. He didn't need the Looking Crystal anymore. The turrets and towers seemed to stab into the sky.

Affren appeared at Tanner's side. "That's Derthsin's lair, isn't it?" he said.

Tanner nodded slowly. "We should take the men closer," he said. "Just out of arrow's range. Follow us."

On foot, with Gwen and Rufus alongside them, Tanner and Affren led the people of Avantia down into the sandy plain in front of the fortress. Every so often, the ground would rumble as the volcano spewed more flames. The black walls seemed to tower over them, and Tanner made out the mutterings of unease in the ranks:

"We can't get in there!"

"Derthsin's too powerful."

"Even with the Beasts, it's suicide!"

Gulkien turned his shaggy head toward Falkor and growled. Clearly the Beasts were anxious, too. Tanner could see the sentries without his Looking Crystal now. More soldiers swelled their ranks, raising their pikes and readying their bows and arrows. Their movements were swift, efficient, as if they were completely unafraid of the army marching toward them.

And why shouldn't they be? Tanner asked himself. *They're safe behind their walls, and they have varkules and real weapons.*

When they were two hundred paces from the fortress, Tanner waved along the line to draw up his troops. Already he could feel the distant heat from the lava. The Avantian soldiers huddled in groups, sharing the last scraps of food they carried with them, or sipped water from their flasks. A few sat down in the grass. The horses tossed their manes and stamped the ground. Affren sat alone, examining his sword blade.

He's thinking of what he's lost, Tanner realized. He could feel the whole army rolling the same question over in their minds. *They've given so much already. Can I really ask them to give more?*

"They're scared," said Gwen.

"Aren't you?" asked Rufus, with a grim smile.

Tanner placed a hand on each of their shoulders, squeezing them tightly. Then he ran over to Firepos, and the flame bird lowered her wing for him to climb. Tanner sat astride her feathers. "Take me up," he said.

Firepos dipped her head and sprang off the ground. Tanner guided her above the crowd. One by one the faces of the people turned upward.

"Wish me luck," he muttered to the flame bird.

Speak from your heart, she replied. *And you will speak true.*

Tanner closed his eyes for a moment. Then, his fists clenched with determination, he shouted down to the watching army.

"People of Avantia! Behind those walls lurks an enemy greater than any we have faced before. You know him well."

"Derthsin!" shouted a man.

"That's right," bellowed Tanner. "His soldiers have ravaged your villages and burned your crops. Many of you have lost loved ones, as I have. Brothers, sisters, mothers, sons. Derthsin has shown no mercy in his quest to take this kingdom as his own."

Firepos beat the air steadily with her wings as the crowd muttered and nodded.

"As individuals, in our scattered villages," Tanner went on, "we're powerless to stand up to his forces. He has weapons of steel, and his soldiers outnumber our own. He has a Beast."

"We have Beasts, too!" Affren called.

Below him, Tanner saw Gulkien shake his head and snarl, while Falkor rippled his scales in a wave of silver and gold, letting his tail thump the ground.

"We have more than that!" called Tanner. "Derthsin's soldiers fight because of fear. You who join me today to take on his army have right on your side. We fight for each other, and to rid this land of Derthsin forever. Only together can we wield our strength."

He paused to catch his breath and steered Firepos around to face the black walls.

"Derthsin seeks a magic this kingdom is better off without," Tanner continued. "If he claims the pieces of the Face of Anoret, if he wears the Mask of Death, he becomes unstoppable. Many will die today, but let's make sure they don't give their blood for nothing. Let's show this monster that Avantia will not fall beneath his boot without a fight." Tanner drew his sword and pointed it at the fortress gates. "Who's with me?"

A long silence descended over the crowd. The villagers looked from one to the other, their weapons on the ground, at their sides, or held limply in their hands. Tanner looked down to Gwen and Rufus. The wizard boy shrugged.

Then, toward the back of the crowd, a young woman carrying a staff rose to her feet.

"I'm with you!" she called.

"Me, too!" yelled an old man with a cracked voice, standing stiffly and clenching a fist over his head.

One after the other, the rest stood, too, and joined their voices until their roar seemed to lift Tanner higher. The soldiers of Avantia brandished their weapons, or hammered their shields until the sound shook the sky. The only face missing from the crowd was Castor's. Firepos let out a screech that lingered on the air.

Tanner's heart swelled with pride. If only his grandmother were here. He imagined her smiling face and knew she, too, would have tied back her gray braids and seized her ax, as she had that day when Gor came to their cottage.

I'll fight for you, Esme, Tanner promised.

He grinned down to Gwen, who nodded with grim satisfaction.

"We're ready," he muttered under his breath, feeling a rush of bloodlust. "Are you, Derthsin?"

As soon as the words left his lips, a low, blaring war horn sounded from the fortress like some enraged creature calling out its anger. The noise burrowed into Tanner's skull so that he had to put his hands to his ears. Falkor hissed below him, his scales taking on the gray sickly hue of anguish. When the sound died, Tanner heard a crack and the rattle of chains. Slowly, like a giant pair of jaws gaping open, the drawbridge in the fortress wall began to descend.

Tanner nudged Firepos forward until she hovered in the air just above Gulkien. The wolf gouged the grass with his paws, his nose wrinkled and eyes narrowed.

"Is Derthsin just going to let us in?" asked Gwen.

"He's expecting us," said Tanner.

The drawbridge thumped down with a mighty crash, forming a steep ramp over the lava moat. Tanner stared into the black orifice beyond. A shape appeared, lit by the flickering orange light from the molten rock below.

"It's a horse," said Rufus, shifting forward a little on Falkor's scales.

The creature lumbered forward, and Tanner saw he was no ordinary steed. Jets of hot breath snorted from his flaring nostrils, and his coat, where he wasn't covered in tough leather plates, was black as the night sky.

Varlot, Firepos said, her wing tips sparking flames.

As the creature emerged from the shadows, Tanner made out General Gor sitting astride the saddle. *My old enemy*, Tanner thought. Gor's shoulders rocked arrogantly as he gripped the reins. Tanner couldn't see his face under the black, dragon-snouted helmet he wore, but he could feel the general's eyes drilling through the slits and resting upon him. The army of villagers behind Tanner drew a gasp of fear.

"Hold firm!" called Tanner.

Varlot's hooves crunched over the boards of the drawbridge, and behind him came the slow trudge of four lines of soldiers, huge brutes in matching armor, carrying oblong shields on their arms and tall pikes in their hands. The shields were marked with white slashes in the shape of a feather.

Firepos's feather! Tanner realized in horror. *The one Derthsin tore from my Beast.*

The flame bird gave an anxious caw of recognition, and Tanner could see what flashed through her mind: the image of Derthsin's body, released from her talons and spiraling into the volcano, one hand clutching a feather from beneath her wing. Tanner reached forward and stroked the scar.

"It's not your fault," he soothed. Firepos could never have known that Derthsin would survive.

The soldiers fanned out in front of the moat, forming ranks across the length of the fortress walls. But still they kept coming from inside, pouring like cockroaches from their hiding places, until the columns swelled ten or a dozen men deep. Men on snarling, hyena-like varkules came last of all, padding between the lines to take their positions in the front. Affren's cavalry horses snorted and stamped.

Gor held up a fist and his army stopped, banging

the stubs of their pikes against the ground as one. Counting across, Tanner guessed there were over two thousand trained soldiers facing their makeshift troops. Varlot continued to pace toward them, as if Gor were challenging Tanner to make the first move. Tanner could sense the evil seeping from every pore of Derthsin's commander. A chilled silence seemed to swallow every sound, and even the horses fell quiet.

Twenty paces away, the general swung off Varlot's back. He stood well away, and Tanner guessed what would happen next.

Varlot snorted and reared up, his hooves churning the air. But instead of falling back to the ground again, his forelegs buckled and thickened, the hooves splitting into anvil-sized fists. The Beast's chest swelled and his hind legs bulged with muscle. Varlot's rear hooves rooted to the ground, growing and taking on a bronze sheen. Their edges glittered, as sharp as the blade of any sword. From the Beast's mouth, a strange, half-choked breath steamed the air as his lips drew back over grinding teeth, and his eyes rolled into the side of his head. With the transformation complete,

Varlot towered three times as tall as Gor now. He'd grown larger every time Tanner saw him, and now he looked almost impossible to control. Even the general seemed uncertain as his companion loomed over him.

Tanner felt a shiver cross his skin. He'd faced Varlot before. *And this will be the last time! I'll make sure of that.*

The Horse Beast stamped his bronze hooves, making the ground shake.

"Remember what I told you," he growled. "I promised I would make you bleed."

"My blood comes at a high price," said Tanner.

Varlot grinned, showing bone-crushing teeth. "Like your Beast's?"

Tanner could suddenly taste Firepos's blood again on his tongue: hot, thick, powerful. He'd inherited his Beast's strength, and now Firepos was weak.

The flame bird sent an urgent message throbbing through Tanner. *Don't think about that now! You're playing into his hands!* She was right.

"I will take you apart, limb by limb," Tanner said in a voice like steel.

Varlot opened his mouth in a throaty bellow: "Not before I destroy you."

There was a flash of movement. A single figure launched himself from the front of the allied line, charging at the Beast. "You killed my wife!" he yelled.

"Affren, no!" Gwen called.

Two more men broke after the villager to pull him back. Affren brandished his sword as he charged straight at Varlot, swinging it wildly. "For vengeance!" he shouted.

Varlot simply swung one of his enormous fists, catching the rebel leader under the chin and snapping back his head. Affren slid across the ground, tripping the two men who had followed. Tanner could see his neck was broken.

The other men picked themselves up and fled back to the lines.

Laughter broke out over the chill silence. Gor folded his arms across his chest. "Who's next?"

An uncontrollable rage surged through Tanner as he looked at the broken body of his comrade. He squeezed with his knees, and Firepos climbed higher.

Gulkien sprang into the air, joining them with thrusts of his sinewy wings. Falkor lifted his head, and his scales glittered an angry scarlet.

General Gor drew his blade — a black, serrated broadsword.

Tanner leaned forward, lifted his sword, then shouted with everything he had.

"Attack!"

CHAPTER 8

The varkules prowled forward, their striped fur pulsing with muscle and their ragged claws extended. They paced ahead of the infantry, snapping drooling jaws. Tanner saw an ax spin through the air and bury itself in one of the creature's chests. Gwen! The varkule collapsed backward, crushing its howling rider.

Gulkien snarled as Gwen pulled another throwing ax from inside her cloak.

The death of an enemy soldier seemed to give the Avantians courage. They pushed on in a wave of war cries, with the cavalry galloping ahead of the charge. At the same time, the enemy broke ranks and rushed forward, past Gor and Varlot. Their weapons met with a deafening clash. Tanner saw a mass of writhing varkules smashing into horses, thrusting and slashing swords. Screams and grunts filled the air. Falkor surged through the throng with Rufus astride his back, seizing a soldier in his fangs and tossing him from side to side until he was dead. His tail scooped up two others and squeezed their life away in his powerful coils while Rufus sent out beams of magic from his fingertips, scorching men or making weapons leap out of soldiers' hands. A clutch of enemies cowered as Gulkien spread his wings over them, descending with his claws outstretched to tear their flesh.

Tanner spotted Gor striding back toward the fortress with Varlot at his side.

"You're not running away from this fight," Tanner muttered. "Let's finish him, Firepos!" he yelled.

The flame bird responded at once, rising up to gather herself. For a moment she hovered, then dipped her golden beak toward the general and his Beast. Drawing her wings to her side, she dove.

Flames sear across my feathers and I drop like an arrow at the Horse Beast who has pledged his loyalty to evil. He turns, his eyes rolling angrily as he lifts his fists to throw me aside. I open my beak with a screech, folding my wings and reaching with my talons. They slip through the cracks in his armor and rip into his flank. I grip tightly as he bellows, sinking my red-hot talons deeper into his flesh.

I hear the clash of metal on metal and see that Tanner leans over my side, swinging his sword against Gor's dragon helmet. The general staggers back but recovers and lunges with his own blade. Tanner deflects the blow and slashes in a blurred arc. The sword catches Gor's arm, sinking into the muscle of his shoulder. The general hisses and spins away. With a single wing beat and a thrust of my legs, I push above them. Varlot sinks to one knee as blood seeps from his wounds over the plates of his armor. His eyes blaze with pain and anger.

"Take me back down!" yells Tanner. "I have to finish him!"

The flames of the lava blind my vision. Something is wrong here, and I wheel away from the fortress.

The army is in danger. I sense it. We must go to them.

Tanner looked back in frustration as the general placed a hand against Varlot's leg to pull himself upright. He couldn't understand why Firepos was taking him away.

"Gor was in my grasp!"

The army needs you, Firepos replied.

Tanner tore his eyes from his foe and surveyed the battle. The allied forces had been pushed back across the scrubby plain, and the ground was littered with the corpses of the dead and the dying. Horses lay on their sides or limped away.

In the center of the battle was Falkor. Several arrows protruded from his scales, but the Beast was still fighting, coiled among a trio of varkules and a small group of Avantians. His black eyes narrowed as he darted at the legs of one of the vicious creatures. It tried to wriggle away, but Falkor yanked back, tearing the limb free.

The enemy troops had kept their shape better than the village forces, but Tanner noticed a spot where Gor's men were only two or three deep. He urged Firepos to swoop over a group of Avantian horsemen. "Form into a row!" he shouted. "Make a charge over there!"

The Avantian cavalry wheeled around and stormed forward, their horses smashing through the line. The foot soldiers followed through, spilling into the empty space behind and attacking the enemy from the rear.

"Tanner! Help!" shouted Gwen.

Tanner turned toward her voice and saw her desperately swinging her rapier at a crowd of enemy soldiers on her right side. Five others had managed to seize Gulkien's left wing so he couldn't fly.

"Help them!" Tanner shouted.

An orange glow formed under Firepos's talons as she swooped. She released it at the band of soldiers keeping Gwen busy, turning them into columns of flames. As Tanner rose again, he saw Gwen set upon the others with her rapier, slashing and stabbing until they released Gulkien's wing. The wolf turned on the ones who remained, savaging them with his teeth.

Tanner and Firepos swept over Rufus, who moved through the battle on foot, blasting bolts of blue light from his staff and spilling enemy soldiers to the left and right. One raised his shield, deflecting the beam of light at the fortress walls. With a crunch, the masonry cascaded into the lava below, incinerating instantly.

A scream sounded beneath him, and Tanner looked down to see a soldier driving back a woman with his pike. She only had a rake to defend herself and stumbled onto her hands and knees. Firepos landed and Tanner leaped off her back, rolling across the ground. As he stood, the soldier raised the pike to impale the woman. Tanner hacked at the soldier's neck with his sword, and he fell with a gurgling cry.

Tanner climbed onto his Beast once more and took to the air. *The tide's turning,* he realized. Only a handful of varkules remained, and many of those hobbled from their wounds. Gradually the Avantians were steadying their lines, holding their own as the enemy numbers thinned. Many lay dead or dying over the plain, and a thousand cries of pain reached his ears.

Without their sacrifice, we wouldn't even have gotten this close, Tanner thought.

"It's time to find Gor," he said to Firepos.

His Beast suddenly banked sideways, dipping dangerously in the air. Tanner had to pull her feathers to keep her steady.

Pain surges like a lightning strike from the old scar beneath my wing. My eyes are turning blind and I trust my rider to guide me. Derthsin is near. His evil poisons the air I breathe, quenching my flames. My wings feel heavy and it's all I can do to stay aloft.

Tanner must not know the agony I suffer. He must focus on the battle ahead. My life is not important anymore, and if he knew this, hopelessness would sap his strength, too.

What's the matter? he asks.

Nothing, I lie. Keep your eyes on the fight, my rider.

Firepos seemed to gather herself and rose up on strong wing thrusts. Tanner felt in control once more as he spotted Gor striding toward a wounded Avantian, who was trying to stand but bleeding heavily from his thigh. Varlot had disappeared. *Perhaps he's mortally wounded*, Tanner dared to hope.

Gor planted a boot on the man's side and pushed him onto his back. He drew his sword, the edge glittering and stained with blood.

"What's it to be?" Gor called to Tanner. "Shall I end his suffering?"

A fireball was too risky. Tanner directed Firepos in a low glide and leaped off midflight, landing a few paces from Derthsin's general. His fist clenched around the hilt of his sword. "Step away from him," he said. "It's me you want."

"You dare to face me, boy?" Gor sneered.

Firepos hovered overhead.

Help the others, Tanner commanded. The flame bird lifted away.

Gor tipped back the face guard of his helmet to reveal his dark features. Tanner drew his sword with an icy hiss from its sheath.

"You killed my grandmother," he said. "I promised myself that day I would see you die."

Gor smiled and swung his blade in a slow figure eight, then snapped down the visor. "I can reunite you with her, if you wish."

Anger pulsed through Tanner's veins, but as he stepped forward, he noticed Rufus come into view a few paces to his right. The wizard was swinging his staff to drive back two enemy soldiers. As he turned, his cloak billowed. The world seemed to slow as Tanner saw the outline of the mask pieces inside. For a moment, he forgot about General Gor completely. His grip on the sword loosened.

Come to me, said a voice. *The Mask of Death calls to you.*

Rufus swiped the end of his staff against the jaw of one of the soldiers and came closer to Tanner. As he did so, the voice in his head grew louder.

Take the mask. Wear it. The power calls to you.

Tanner turned just in time to see Gor swinging his sword. He stepped aside as the edge bit into the ground. Gor lashed at him with the back of his gauntleted hand, sending Tanner sprawling across the ground. Tanner shook his head clear and climbed to his feet dizzily. As he did, he felt the draw of the mask nearby. Beyond Gor, a varkule closed its jaws over a prone villager's throat. Bloodlust prickled over Tanner's skin at the sight. *This won't go on!* he promised himself.

He threw himself at Gor, taking him by surprise and driving the hilt of his sword into the general's face. He collapsed full-length like a felled tree, blood pouring from both nostrils.

Tanner lifted his sword to deliver the final blow, but something dragged his eyes away.

The mask! Rufus was just a few paces away. *It's right there. I could take it. . . .*

Gor scrambled to get up from the ground, picking up a nearby severed arm. As Tanner turned to face him, the General threw it at his chest. Tanner ducked and battered the limb away.

Gor regained his feet.

"Your mind's not on the battle," he leered, eyes gleaming triumphantly behind the slits of his helmet. "My master was right. You're thinking of another prize." He slashed at Tanner, who met the blade with his own in a shower of sparks. The blow jarred Tanner's shoulder painfully, but he stood his ground. Part of him knew he should counter, but with the mask so close, he could barely concentrate. Gor lunged again, and Tanner blocked low, driving the general's sword tip into the ground.

"Impressive!" growled the general. "Your sword skills have improved, Tanner. Anyone would think you had tasted a Beast's blood."

His words penetrated the fog of Tanner's brain. Rage took over, and he rushed at Gor.

The general stepped aside, seizing Tanner's sword arm, and thrust out a foot to trip him. As Tanner fell on his back, he felt his sword being twisted deftly from his hand. Gor stood over him, the point of his blade leveled at Tanner's chest. He lifted the face guard again and grinned. Spots of blood from his nose dripped over the front of his breastplate.

"Tell me," he sneered, "which part of you shall I remove first?"

CHAPTER 9

General Gor pulled back his blade, dark clouds swirling beyond him. Tanner waited for the serrated edge to sink into his chest.

But the general's face creased in a smile as something seemed to occur to him. "Perhaps I won't kill you quite yet," he goaded, kicking the toe of his boot into Tanner's side so that his ribs thrummed with pain. Tanner rolled onto his side, groaning, and another fierce kick to his kidneys made him writhe in the mud.

The general knelt beside him, holding the point of Tanner's own sword against his cheek. The tip pressed harder and harder against his skin until red-hot pain blossomed across his face, making his eyes water. He licked his lips and tasted the salt tang of blood. General

Gor was pressing the sword so hard now that Tanner could feel its point against his teeth. He couldn't speak and he dare not fight back.

"You were never going to get the better of me," the general said, bringing his face close to Tanner's. "Boys and their pets should know when they've met their match."

Gor pulled the blade free and shoved Tanner onto his back again. Tanner felt blood trickling down his throat and he swallowed hard. His enemy lifted the sword in both hands above his head, ready to strike it down into Tanner's heart.

But the general's body shuddered and his eyes suddenly widened. His face twisted, his brow creasing into a look of confusion. An odd gurgling escaped his open lips, followed by a thin trickle of red-stained saliva. He jolted again as if waking from a doze, and the point of a sword pushed through the armor on his chest. With a strangled moan, the general looked down as the rest of the blade broke through. His own sword clattered from his hand and his eyes rolled back. Slowly, the general began to tip forward.

Tanner rolled out of the way as Gor's body smashed face-first into the ground, the blade pulling free. A familiar face looked down at the sword with grim satisfaction.

"Castor!" said Tanner.

His old friend breathed heavily, his broad chest rising and falling. He wore no armor, and his clothes were spattered with blood.

"You didn't think I'd miss this, did you?" Castor said, wiping his sword on the back of Gor's cloak. "I couldn't risk you messing up all my well-laid plans." He offered his hand.

Tanner took it and stumbled to his feet. The smile faded from Castor's face as his old friend gazed at Tanner's cheek.

"Here," he said, reaching into his tunic and pulling out an old rag. "Hold this against the wound. Press hard."

"How bad is it?" Tanner managed to ask.

Castor shrugged. "A pinprick!" His laughter died away. "Seriously, though. It's not as bad as it probably feels; it could have been a lot worse. The bleeding will stop soon. Nera found you," he added, nodding past Tanner.

Tanner turned to see the giant cat leaping through the mass of soldiers, lashing with her claws. One of Gor's men twisted with a scream. Nera growled and pounced, closing her mouth over the arm of another and ripping him in two.

"She didn't want to miss out, either," said Castor with the hint of a smile.

The battle still raged in various parts of the field, with Gwen guiding Gulkien in low swoops over the enemy soldiers, the flying wolf snatching them up in his jaws and throwing them back to earth. Firepos hurled a rolling fireball at a line of soldiers, scattering them in a shower of flames, and Falkor plunged his fangs through the back of a soldier before hurling the body over his head.

Tanner scanned the battlefield until he saw Rufus, sheltered behind the carcass of a varkule while archers fired from the walls. Every so often he leaned out and cast another bolt of energy at the walls, blasting the bowmen back or spilling them into the moat to meet a fiery end. He leaped onto a rock and his blue shirt billowed against his chest. His shoulders were pulled back as he sent more bolts of magic from his fingertips, his eyes dark with intent.

That isn't the boy who cowered in a cave, Tanner thought, holding the rag to his cheek. Rufus was changing before his eyes, becoming a warrior with strong magic. He twirled his staff in his hands and rammed one end of it into a soldier's chest, so that he fell to the ground. A bolt of blue light followed, blasting the man's armor from his limbs, and there was a sudden flash of movement as Falkor descended on the man, jaws closing around his ribs. There was a snapping sound and Tanner turned away.

How many more soldiers lurked inside the castle? There was no more time for mopping up blood. Tanner seized his sword and lifted his arm to summon Firepos. The flame bird dropped the enemy soldier she was carrying into a group of his comrades and wheeled around to fly to her rider.

Tanner punched Castor on the arm. "You saved my life," he said.

Castor smiled meekly. "You'll have a nice scar to show for your troubles, though," he said, nodding at

Tanner's wound. "I don't expect you to forgive me. I acted like a coward. I . . ."

Tanner shook his head. "You don't need to explain. You're here now."

Castor's grin widened. "Well, you could hardly manage without your best swordsman!" He lowered his eyes. "And besides, I missed you three."

Firepos landed beside Tanner and nudged Castor aside with a wing.

"It's all right," said Tanner, laying a hand on her beak.

Your face . . . Firepos sent an anxious message to him.

"It's nothing. A flesh wound," Tanner said, willing the Beast not to ask any more questions. Gripping the scruffy, dense feathers behind her neck, Tanner heaved himself onto the flame bird's back. The ground shook with a deep rumbling as she sprang into the air and wheeled over the clashing armies. Tanner's eyes were drawn upward to the volcano's crater, where sparks exploded into the air. Great, roiling clouds of purple smoke billowed out and poured menacingly down the slope toward the fortress.

"Derthsin's angry," muttered Tanner.

I wheel about on tired wings and release a series of sharp caws to alert my fellow Beasts. Gulkien's muzzle snaps around, matted with the blood of our foes. Falkor draws himself in a coil of shimmering silver, and Nera's eyes blaze as orange as the lava itself. She roars to me, her hot blood pulsing through her muscles, her fangs dripping gore.

The first battle is over, I tell them. But the war is far from won.

Tanner saw the other Beasts break away. Falkor slithered toward Rufus, and Nera padded over the carpet of dead bodies to Castor's side. Gwen, kneeling to pull one of her throwing axes loose of a soldier's neck, mounted Gulkien. Only pockets of the enemy remained, and many had laid down their weapons already as the odds turned against them. Here and there, brave Avantians cornered the remnants of the enemy or sank exhausted to the ground. Firepos tossed her head, and her eyes glinted like burning embers.

Trust us, she said.

"Let the Beasts guide you!" Tanner shouted to his friends.

With the other three Beasts behind her, Firepos glided down toward the approach to the fortress. She sailed on the baking air, over the corpse of General Gor.

"I hope you're watching, Esme," Tanner muttered.

At the foot of the drawbridge, Firepos suddenly tipped her wings and angled her body upward, soaring like an arrow toward the dark gateway through which the soldiers had emerged. Tanner crouched close to her feathers, the hot wind blasting through his clothes. The pain in his face had almost faded away.

It's time to face our destiny, the flame bird said.

They rushed through the gateway and darkness swallowed them. Though Tanner blinked he could see only shadows as they soared through a tunnel. He felt Firepos's wings thumping up and down. Her muscles twitched, making tiny adjustments to her flight, and he realized they were flying upward at a slight gradient. The air pressed heavy and hot all around him like a smothering hand, and it was hard not to let panic take over in the blackness.

From behind he heard the soft draft of Gulkien's wings and Nera's padding paws. Only Falkor could truly see, surely. He was used to a life in the darkness of caves. Were the rest of the Beasts charging blind?

The ancient power of the Fates guides us, Firepos reassured Tanner.

Tanner gripped her flanks tightly with his knees and picked out a faint orange glow ahead. As the light grew stronger he saw the rocks around them, just shadows flitting past. Gradually he could make out stone walls. Here and there he saw marks left by pickaxes and chisels.

"I think this place is man-made," he shouted to Gwen.

"It's getting warmer, too," she answered. "It must be a passage to the heart of the volcano!"

This fortress wasn't here then, Firepos sent the message back to Tanner. *He must have built this after he survived plunging down into the volcano's depths.*

It was unbelievable. During all the years Tanner had been growing up, Derthsin had been within walking distance. Biding his time, watching, waiting, ensconced in a heart of fire.

The tunnel suddenly opened up and a blast of heat nearly knocked Tanner from Firepos's back. He gasped at the vista laid out before him. A huge cavern loomed over a pit of boiling lava. The molten rock seethed and bubbled with black and red swirls, and geysers of fire spouted from the surface, falling back again in hissing splashes. Purple smoke spiraled up through cracks in the domed roof, where stalactites reached down like withered fingers.

Firepos hovered as the other Beasts broke into the cavern. Gulkien landed first on the banks of the lava pit, and the orange heat showed through his stretched wings, picking out the network of red capillaries within. Nera crouched, her head lowered between her jutting shoulders, ready to pounce at any danger, and Falkor, his scales reflecting the lava's golden shimmer, edged forward, flickering his tongue nervously.

"Look!" said Gwen, pointing. Her face glowed red in the fiery reflection of the lava.

Tanner and the others turned to where she indicated. A rocky platform reached out over the side of the boiling lava pool, approached by two paths, one from each side of the cavern. At the opposite end of the platform, a strange stone podium jutted upward to head height. Tanner strained his eyes through the blurred heat and saw a figure limping slowly toward the podium, shrouded in a bloodred cloak and hood. He reached the end of the shelf, just a footstep away from falling into the lava, and stopped. Tanner's skin suddenly felt cold, despite the heat. It was a figure he'd seen before in Gor's enchanted fire. A figure who had haunted his dreams since the day he drove a sword through Tanner's father.

"Derthsin," he whispered.

The stooped figure pushed back his hood with a bone-white hand. Tanner made out long fingers ending in cracked yellow nails. The bare scalp beneath was white, too, as if Derthsin had never been out in the sunlight. Ridges of scarred flesh marked his head, puckering the skin of half his face. Deep-set eyes, blacker than coal, watched from beneath a heavy brow. Derthsin grinned, and his thin, bloodless lips parted.

"Welcome, Beast Riders," he hissed, darting a red tongue through his brown teeth. "I've been expecting you." His eyes flickered over the wound on Tanner's face. "I see you met Gor on your way over here."

"And killed him!" Castor spat back.

Derthsin reached into his cloak and pulled free the final piece of the mask — the spiked section from the left side of the lower jaw. He positioned it on top of the podium facing Tanner and his friends.

"The rest is near," said Derthsin. "I sense it."

"You'll never have it!" yelled Tanner. He urged Firepos forward, and the flame bird dove toward the platform. Derthsin lifted a hand, palm outward, and Tanner saw the mark of the flame bird's feather burned into the skin. Firepos screeched and drew up her wings. A wave of vibration, like a wall of wind, shook Tanner's body as the two of them were thrown backward.

"You think you can attack *me*?" said Derthsin.

Firepos managed to right herself and landed beside Gulkien.

"Your Beasts are like helpless insects to me," continued Derthsin, pointing at each of them. "Soon the mask will be mine, and Anoret will rise again! All the Beasts of Avantia will be under my thrall, and the people of this kingdom will cower at my feet."

"Never!" shouted Tanner. "Surround him!"

The others guided their Beasts from the edge of the cavern, fanning out to face Derthsin in a semicircle.

"Pathetic!" shouted the evil lord. He raised both hands, and a curtain of lava shot up from the pool. It surged toward them, then showered down. Firepos thrust upward with her wings, dodging the spatter of molten rock. The other Beasts swerved away, too, but Falkor wasn't quick enough. Drips of lava rained over his scales, burning away patches in hissing columns of smoke. Rufus's Beast squirmed in agony, then drew himself into a coil.

"Your foolish Beast shouldn't have dropped me down here," said Derthsin to Tanner, spreading his arms wide to take in the cavern. "It took me years to master the flames, but I was patient."

Falkor's eyes closed, as if he had fallen unconscious.

"Rufus, can you heal him?" asked Gwen, nodding toward Falkor's scorched coils.

But Rufus didn't answer, and seemed to smile. He slipped from Falkor's back and edged along the cavern wall to one of the pathways leading to Derthsin's platform. His eyes were black as coal, unreadable, and a smile spread across his face that sent shivers down Tanner's spine. His hands hung at his sides, their magic useless now.

"Rufus, no!" Castor shouted, failing to understand what Tanner had realized. "You can't take him on alone."

Dread seeped through Tanner when Rufus didn't even turn.

"He's enchanted," he told the others.

At his words, Rufus turned and glared at him, his eyes rimmed orange from the flames. He drew his lips back in a snarl and raised his staff in warning.

I have to get to the pieces of the mask before he gives them to Derthsin! Tanner started to run toward Rufus, but an arc of lava rose from the pit and splattered across his path, blocking the way. He shrank back from the molten rock.

"I wouldn't interfere, if I were you," cackled Derthsin. He watched Rufus make his way around the rim of the lava pool. "Don't you see?" he said. "The mask *wants* to be with me. Destiny brings the Face of Anoret together again."

"Come back, Rufus!" shouted Gwen, her voice choked with tears.

Rufus turned to her, his eyes as dead as stones. "Leave me be!" Then he stepped onto the stone platform.

"That's right! Come to your master!" called Derthsin. "The power of the mask cannot be denied."

Rufus took the edges of his blue cloak and roughly tore it open. Tanner swallowed thickly and wanted to look away. The young wizard pulled out the three pieces of the mask they'd found so far.

So many died to find those, Tanner thought. *And for what?*

Derthsin held out his arms, and Rufus placed the leather sections into his arms.

It's over, Tanner thought.

CHAPTER 10

Derthsin's eyes glittered as he gazed at the pieces of the mask, then positioned them on the podium alongside the other fragment. He reached out with pale fingers and stroked Rufus's cheek with a grime-caked nail.

"You've done well, my friend," he said.

His friend?

Tanner didn't understand. After all they'd been through! Rufus had stood by them, fighting side by side, blasting at the defenses while his Beast attacked the enemy soldiers. . . .

Cold fury swept over Tanner as he realized the truth. Rufus hadn't been trying to destroy the defenses — he'd been trying to get in, to reach Derthsin.

"How long?" he called out. "How long have you been working for him?"

Rufus hunched his shoulders and gazed around at Tanner, his face pale despite the heat. His tongue darted out from between his lips, like a snake's. "From the beginning," Rufus said. "Since he lived back in the cave."

"But we trusted you," gasped Gwen. "All that time you were an enemy in our midst?"

Rufus smiled. "Don't think of me as an enemy, Gwen," he said. "More a . . . negotiator."

"You're a filthy traitor!" shouted Castor. "You can be tossed in a pit of writhing snakes for all I care!"

Rufus raised his eyebrows and lifted his staff. "Careful, Castor. I'll turn *you* into a snake if you don't hold your tongue."

First Geffen, now Rufus, thought Tanner desperately. Where the mask was concerned, no one could be trusted. Could he even trust himself to resist its power?

"Enough!" bellowed Derthsin. "It is time to begin!"

He thrust a hand out toward Tanner and a beam of fire shot from his fingertips like a whip. Tanner lifted his arms to protect his face and felt the tip slice through his sleeve. He looked at his arm and saw a red, raw burn mark on the skin. Derthsin flicked his wrist again and a trail of fire snaked around Tanner's ankle, tugging him from Firepos's back. His Beast screeched as he landed with a heavy thud on the ground. Through his breathlessness, Tanner felt searing pain climb his lower leg. Derthsin pulled, hand over hand, dragging Tanner forward. The stone floor tore at his clothes and scraped the skin on his back. However much he wriggled, he couldn't free himself.

Derthsin grinned, and his lips glistened. "Come to me, Tanner," he hissed. "Soon you will taste real pain!"

I cannot let this happen! My Chosen Rider and I have been through too much.

Nera! I need you to distract our foe.

The giant cat pricks her ears and snatches up a loose boulder in her teeth. With a flick of her head, she hurls it toward Derthsin. As the evil lord dodges aside, I take to the air. The ache under my wing feels like iron hooks tearing at my flesh, but I give three strong beats and dart at my enemy. With a slice of my beak, I cut a gash in his head.

Derthsin's rope of fire dissolves into ash as he stumbles back with a cry of pain. One hand staunches the flow of blood from his head while the other shoots a beam of fire toward me. I turn my feathers and soak up the heat.

Fool! Fire is my friend, as it is yours. You cannot harm me that way!

Tanner limps toward me, and I crouch beside him to let him take his place once more.

"You're too late!" shouted Derthsin, his pale skin smeared with blood. "Rufus, fulfill your destiny!"

As Gulkien and Nera rushed toward Derthsin, carrying their riders, Rufus touched the tip of his staff to the mask with a trembling hand. Nera pounced, covering twenty paces in a single bound, and Castor lifted his sword to strike at the evil lord. A dazzling light, as bright as a bolt of lightning, shot out of Rufus's staff and lit up the cave. Tanner squeezed his eyes shut, but even then he could see the silhouette of the mask, its pieces fusing together along jagged lines. It was much larger now.

"Behold, the Face of Anoret!" bellowed Derthsin.

The light faded and a huge boom rocked the cave, throwing Tanner from Firepos's feathers and driving Gulkien and Nera onto the stone platform. The wolf skidded across the rocks, his wings tangling beneath him and Gwen clinging desperately to his back. Gulkien's claws skittered across the ground, finally dragging him to a halt just short of the edge of the pit. Rufus lay beside the podium, unconscious or dead.

Castor, low against Nera's bristling fur, gazed at Tanner in shock. "What was *that*?"

Derthsin seized the mask from the ground. He held it up to the wall behind him.

"Come, Anoret! Your master calls you!"

The wall shuddered and cracks opened in its surface, snaking up and down. Tanner stared. A huge section of the wall wasn't formed from black rock like the rest of the cavern, but a deep blue stone, stained with dark red streaks. One section started to bulge out, and a three-pronged claw broke away, grasping at the air. An arm, thick as the trunk of an oak, jerked from the wall, and the outline of a torso pressed through.

144

A massive, skeletal head, shaped like a lizard's, shook free of the rock face. Three rows of jagged teeth lined gaping jaws. More of the Beast followed — a stumplike leg ending in scything black claws, and part of her back, lined with silver spikes. She pounded the cavern floor with a thump of her thrashing tail. Anoret stood at least three times as tall as Firepos, with dark blue scales and a red stripe spreading from the back of her head and down her back. The Beast filled the cavern with a roar that shook Tanner's bones.

My old friend, transformed. I recognize Anoret by her eyes, but her soul has nothing left to say to me. I remember when I, Nera, Falkor, and Gulkien blended our blood together to make her stronger, but now she is under the thrall of Derthsin. I beseech you, Anoret — free yourself. My time is drawing to an end, but there is hope left for you. Shake off your shackles and turn your back on this evil master.

I listen for a response, but there is none. She doesn't hear — or chooses not to. There is nothing left I can do.

Tanner struggled not to retch when the glow from the lava pool illuminated Anoret's face. It was nothing but a murky brown mass of rotten, featureless flesh that quivered and twitched with sinew and muscle. Red eyeballs rotated on stalks as the Beast roared in fury, bringing showers of rock debris from the roof of the cavern.

The Beast's face was torn away years ago, Tanner realized. *Just like Firepos told me.*

Anoret struggled to free the left side of her body, moaning as she tried to emerge completely.

Derthsin lifted the mask up toward his own face.

"Come, my loyal creature!" said the evil lord. "Victory is ours!"

If Derthsin puts the mask on, thought Tanner, *it's all over!*

He bent to his side and picked up a rock the size of his fist. Drawing back his arm, he hurled it at Derthsin. It caught his elbow and Derthsin lowered his arms with a snarl of anger. He shot a bolt of fire at Tanner, who dodged aside, then ran at his enemy.

"Don't let Derthsin put on the mask!" shouted Tanner.

Gwen snatched an ax from her belt and sent it spinning toward Derthsin. The evil lord moved quickly, twisting away and drawing his own sword, a black-jeweled blade. He deflected the ax, which skittered off across the stone.

Tanner ran from one side, taking the stone pathway to the platform, and Castor took the other. Derthsin cast a beam of fire that exploded on the ground by Castor's feet, making him stumble back. Next he threw one at Tanner. Lifting his sword, Tanner deflected it harmlessly against the cavern wall, and slashed downward at Derthsin. The evil lord tried to back away, but the sword tip nicked his shoulder.

"There's another scar for your collection!" said Tanner. He lunged, but Derthsin smashed his blade aside. Tanner drove a foot into Derthsin's stomach, and the mask flew from his hand.

"No!" roared the evil lord. Tanner watched the mask skid toward the edge of the platform, gleaming orange in the lava light. A hot surge pulsed through his veins.

I can't lose the power. . . .

He rushed to claim it, but something snagged his ankle and he fell face-first. Derthsin clawed his way over Tanner's body.

"It's mine!" Derthsin hissed.

Tanner rolled over dizzily and tasted blood on his lips. He saw Derthsin reach for the mask on all fours and bring it toward his face. Tanner jumped up, landing on Derthsin's back. As Derthsin staggered to his feet, trying to pull the mask on, Tanner seized Derthsin's wrists and pushed it away from his face with all his strength.

"I won't let you. . . ." Tanner muttered.

Finally, Derthsin twisted and threw Tanner over his shoulder. Tanner teetered on the edge of the fiery pit as the mask spun out of his hands toward the lava.

"No!" Derthsin screamed, turning his wild eyes on Tanner. "Burn, you pathetic Avantian!" The evil lord's foot lashed out and struck him in the chest.

Tanner tumbled over the edge after the Mask of Death. He rushed down toward the bubbling pool, his arms and legs flailing. His fingers brushed a rock jutting from the wall of the fiery pit and he grabbed it, his arm screaming in its socket as it broke his fall. Heat blistered his fingertips as he clung desperately.

The mask splashed into the lava, glowing red-hot, then white-hot. Thick lava bubbled up through the eye sockets as it sank from sight.

Tanner felt as if he had been whipped all over his body. The heat was unbearable.

He closed his eyes as his fingers slid from the rock.

CHAPTER 11

Something closed around his waist, and his body jarred to a halt. He tried to open his eyes, but the heat seared his eyeballs. The bitter stench of singed hair filled his nostrils, and he realized it was his own. Then Tanner felt himself being lifted away from the lava. His hands found Firepos's talons, and he managed to look up and see the feathered belly of his Beast.

Firepos turned in the air, and Tanner saw Derthsin crouched at the edge of the platform, his head in his hands as he looked at where the mask had fallen. Castor and Gwen waited on their Beasts, watching with their weapons brandished as Anoret peeled her second leg loose from the rock face.

"The mask is gone!" shouted Tanner from Firepos's claws. "It's over, Derthsin!"

The evil lord stood up and gathered his scarlet cape around him. The scars on his face glowed livid pink as rage pulsed through him.

"It's not over until you die!" he roared, casting a bolt of black flame toward Tanner. Firepos shifted in the air, dropping a fraction, and the beam slammed into her wing. She shrieked and threw Tanner clear. He landed in a heap on a rocky ledge and watched in horror as the flame bird fluttered erratically, fighting to stay aloft with her damaged wing half extended. She managed to reach the ledge and sank down beside him, her eyes wild with pain.

"Firepos!" said Tanner, trying to see the wound.

It's nothing, she said.

Tanner knew from the way her body sagged on one side that she was lying. "Let me see," he said.

But when he tried to reach toward her, she moved away.

My wing is broken, replied his Beast. *There's nothing to be done.*

"But there must be something . . ." Tanner began, trailing off as he realized the flame bird spoke the

151

truth. A feeling of grief, hard as a punch, landed in the pit of his stomach.

Tanner's voice caught in his throat. "It's because I drank your blood, isn't it?" he said hoarsely. "You can't heal yourself anymore."

Firepos's eyes were soft, and she stroked his cheek with the side of her beak.

Tears welled up into Tanner's eyes. If the flame bird couldn't fight, she had no chance of surviving at all.

"I won't let this happen!" he shouted.

The Fates decide, said Firepos.

With a draft of his leathered wings, Gulkien dropped onto the ledge beside them, sniffing at Firepos's feathers. Nera pounced up, too, nudging the flame bird with her muzzle.

"Thought you might need this," said Castor, handing Tanner his sword.

"Firepos is injured," said Tanner, stroking the downy feathers above her beak. "She can't fly."

Across the cavern, Anoret roared, smashing the ground with her tail in an effort to pull free her arm.

"We don't have long," said Gwen. "We have to fight, Tanner."

The flame bird cawed softly and pushed Tanner away with a gentle shove of her beak.

"What are you doing?" asked Tanner, as she raised herself up weakly.

What I must, she replied, turning to face Derthsin.

"No!" shouted Tanner. "You can't!"

But Firepos pushed herself off the ledge, keeping herself aloft with her one good wing. Derthsin grinned and raised his arms as she angled her talons forward.

"It's time to finish what we started, all those years ago," said Derthsin. "Time you suffered as I did."

Firepos's eyes glinted with newfound determination, but Tanner could hardly bear to watch. She sent him a final message:

Farewell, my Chosen Rider. You will always be with me.

She dove at Derthsin as he fired a black beam. It caught her in the middle of her gleaming breast feathers, blasting her across the cavern. Tanner saw the light fade from the flame bird's eyes as she fell into the lava. Her body sank beneath the surface.

Tanner rushed forward, arms outstretched and mouth gaping wordlessly. He felt Gwen and Castor grip his shoulders to pull him back, and struggled against them.

"No! No! Please!" he choked.

"She's gone," Castor muttered.

Tanner's knees buckled and he collapsed, his chest racked with sobs. *This can't be happening*, he thought. *Firepos can't be dead.*

Derthsin's cackle made him wipe his eyes. "We have visitors!" said the evil lord.

At the entrance to the cavern Varlot stamped into view, his chest heaving, his armor gouged and stained with dried blood. At his back stood a clutch of soldiers, escaped from the battlefield outside. Two rode snarling varkules.

The evil Beast's eyes fell on Derthsin. In his low growl, he said, "My master . . . General Gor is . . ."

"I felt his spirit perish," sneered Derthsin. "He has let me down for the last time."

With a crunching sound, Anoret finally tore free from the rock face. Her eyes swiveled onto Derthsin,

154

and for a moment, Tanner saw fear in the sorcerer's eyes. The men behind Varlot cowered in terror.

Anoret lumbered across the cavern in giant strides until she towered over Derthsin. Her thick tail swayed menacingly back and forth and her dark blue skin gave out an eerie glow.

The giant Beast looked first at Derthsin, then at Varlot, and finally at Tanner and his friends.

"Now the mask is destroyed, whose side will she take?" whispered Castor.

"We can't wait to find out," said Gwen, gripping Tanner's shoulder to pull him up. "We have to fight!"

Tanner shook his head. "Fight who? What's the point? Firepos is dead."

Gwen's hand caught his face in a slap, jolting him to his senses. "Firepos is dead, but you still have us. Don't let her death be in vain."

Tanner was glad the flickering light of the lava concealed his deep flush of shame. "You're right," he said. "Let's finish this!"

Tanner gripped his sword and jumped down from the rocky ledge. He ran at Varlot, screaming a war cry.

Varlot lifted his own blade and slashed sideways. Tanner dropped into a roll and came up beneath him, slicing through the tendons of one stocky ankle. Varlot tipped back his head in a snort of pain and toppled sideways.

A shadow fell over Tanner, and his eyes climbed the massive shape of Anoret. Tanner ducked as a hand swooped down. He darted between the giant Beast's legs and turned to see her clutching a varkule in one hand, its rider hanging from the stirrups. As if they weighed nothing, Anoret threw them the width of the cavern. They crunched against the far wall and slid to the ground, leaving a bloody smear. Tanner's stomach felt hollow with fear. *This Beast is crazy with grief. . . .* He'd sensed Firepos appealing to her, and Anoret had ignored the flame bird.

A hiss made Tanner's head snap around, and a shape darted from the wall.

Falkor!

The serpent Beast slithered quickly across the ground and wrapped himself around Anoret's leg, closing his coils tightly. The mighty Beast clawed at his scales, pulling herself free with one claw. Falkor raised his body upward, darting his fangs at Anoret's face, but the larger Beast hurled him casually aside.

Nera stalked forward bravely, growling at Anoret. She crouched on her haunches, ready to spring, but the giant Beast swung her massive tail and swept her legs away.

"Nera!" shouted Castor, breaking off from where he clashed with three soldiers, sword on sword, near the entrance to the cavern. Blood seeped from a wound high on his arm.

Tanner twisted to see Gulkien rake his claws into the remaining varkule, but an enemy soldier drove a pike deep into the wolf's hindquarters. Gulkien snarled and kicked the soldier away, but the pike remained, jutting from his side.

This is getting desperate, thought Tanner, plunging his sword into a soldier. As he did so, he saw Derthsin aim a bolt of fire toward him. With the blade still lodged in his enemy's torso, he twisted around, shielding himself with the dying soldier. Flames exploded over the body and Tanner backed away, yanking his blade free. *We're all going to die down here unless we get out soon.*

Two more soldiers approached him, eyes gleaming with bloodlust. The first lunged in, and Tanner smashed his blade away, then swung wildly at the other. Tanner was panting, his sword arm like lead. The soldiers smiled, moving in as one.

Suddenly, the lava in the crater hissed. All faces turned as a shower of fiery sparks burst from the surface. The soldiers in front of Tanner seemed to forget about him and cowered in fear. Even Derthsin lowered his arms and peered into the flames. Tanner saw a shape forming beneath the lava. Two wings . . .

"What is it?" gasped Gwen.

Firepos's golden beak shot from the molten rock, followed by her body, plumage afire. Flames flickered and dripped off her feathers as she climbed majestically from the lava. Her sparkling talons clutched the Mask of Death. She flew in tight circles, climbing higher and higher, sending down a shower of sparks from her feathers.

Tanner watched, his jaw hanging open. She swooped toward him and with a cry of triumph scooped him up in a claw and flung him onto her back so that he nestled between her feathers. Immediately she soared higher again. Tanner had thought he'd lost his companion forever; now he watched over the crown of her head as they flew together. He could feel his heartbeat settling into the same pattern as hers. Reaching down her side, he felt beneath her wing. The old scar had gone.

"That's why you needed to come here!" Tanner called out to her. "You had the power to be reborn!"

So the phoenix emerges from the flames, her voice boomed, strong inside his head. *So life begins again. Justice will find the Mighty.*

With a screech of triumph, Firepos flew down and Tanner scrambled off her back. She dropped the mask from her beak. Instinctively, he held out his hands to catch it, only realizing too late that it would be red-hot.

But it wasn't! The mask felt oddly cool in his grasp and seemed to quiver beneath his fingers. Delicious power crept up his arms, seeped across his chest, and wrapped itself around his heart. .

Gwen rushed to his side. "Tanner, put it on!"

He turned the mask over in his hands. The skin across his face tingled, and all the aches and pains across his body seemed to fade away, leaving only a sense of raw energy, almost too much to take. "I don't know if I should."

"Put it on now!" yelled Castor.

Tanner tore his eyes from the mask and saw his friends' anxious faces. Beyond them, Anoret had turned her red gaze on him. The Beast's eyes settled on the mask, and with a growl, the huge Beast stepped toward them. Tanner and his friends retreated until their backs met the wall of the cavern.

"She looks angry. . . ." said Gwen.

Derthsin strode toward Tanner, his arms outstretched and his cloak whipping behind him. "The mask is mine!" he roared. "Give it to me!"

Tanner made his choice. He lifted the mask to his face.

CHAPTER 12

The fiery cavern faded to gray at the edges, and Tanner's vision blurred. But as he turned his head, everything directly in front of his eyes sharpened to almost painful clarity. He saw details normally invisible to him: the tiniest flecks of saliva around a dead varkule's muzzle; the individual hairs bristling between Gulkien's claws; the beads of sweat rolling down Derthsin's scarred cheek.

"It's incredible!" Tanner gasped.

Anoret stopped ten paces from Tanner and his friends, her chest heaving and her claws relaxed. The fury that had shrouded her seemed to slip away, and a voice penetrated Tanner's mind, as though he were hearing it underwater.

What is your bidding?

Tanner looked into the pitiful face of the ancient Beast, at the flesh empty of features.

You're not evil, are you?

Anoret sighed through the slashes of her nostrils. *I am cursed*, she said. *I obey the one who wears the face torn from me. Derthsin tricked me and took it many years ago, and I have been under his command ever since. Now it is the Mask of Death, and the wearer controls me until I am released.*

I have only one task for you, said Tanner. He raised a hand and pointed to Derthsin.

Very well, Master, Anoret replied, and turned to face the evil lord of Avantia.

Derthsin backed away along the ledge. "No," he muttered. "You're *my* Beast, remember?"

Anoret strode toward him, her huge feet shaking the ground. With two arm thrusts, Derthsin fired black beams toward the Beast, but they bounced off her chest harmlessly.

"Stop her!" shouted Derthsin, tripping over his cloak and landing on his back. Anoret stooped down and seized him in her claws. Derthsin squirmed as he was lifted high over the lava pit. His eyes locked with Tanner's over the Beast's shoulder. He grinned. "Fire is my home, Avantian! Or have you forgotten?"

"I know that," Tanner muttered. "You're not going in the fire."

Anoret tipped back her head and opened her jaws, lifting Derthsin slowly toward the rows of jagged teeth.

"No!" screamed the evil lord. "No! Please! No!"

The Beast's teeth crunched through Derthsin's chest. Tearing the lower half of his body away, Anoret dropped it into the lava. Her jaws worked rhythmically over the rest.

Beside the Beast, Rufus sat up, rubbing his head. He looked around and shuffled backward in alarm when he saw Anoret. "What? What's happening?"

Through the mask, Tanner saw every detail of his confused face. There was no malice there any longer.

"The enchantment's ended," he told the others. "Rufus! Join us!"

Falkor hissed with joy, his scales taking on all the rippling colors of the rainbow. But as Rufus tried to step from the platform, the ground shook more violently, knocking him over again. Tanner had to clutch Gwen to steady himself. Varlot struggled to his feet, and the remaining soldiers looked to the roof anxiously. Only Anoret didn't seem concerned and stood with her feet firmly planted over the rocky shelf.

"What now?" said Castor.

From the center of the lava pool exploded a burst of molten rock. More columns of lava shot up toward the crater, and the cavern's ceiling began to collapse. Boulders the size of Tanner's head broke away and smashed on the ground. He covered his face against the flying shards.

"The volcano's erupting!" said Gwen. "We have to get out!"

Falkor slithered toward Rufus and plucked him up gently in his jaws, then placed him over his back. Castor jumped onto Nera and the Beast purred from deep in her throat. Firepos lowered a wing for Tanner. He'd never been more grateful to take his place astride the burnished, deep brown feathers of her neck. Flames rippled all the way along the feathers of her tail, and she seemed to swell to a size even greater than before.

Her eyes reflected the red glow of the lava, as the molten rock in the pit bubbled and burst, filling the air with a bitter smoke that made Tanner's own eyes water.

The wall from which Anoret had emerged cracked and crumbled into it, sending a wave of molten rock lapping up the edge of the crater.

Cracks opened up throughout the floor of the cavern, snaking close to Gulkien's paws. The wolf took flight as lava seeped through the splits. One chasm opened up in front of the tunnel entrance, widening until it was five, then ten paces across. The enemy soldiers, realizing they'd soon be trapped on an island of rock, rushed this way and that, getting in one another's way. The varkule leaped up at the cavern wall as the ground broke beneath it. For a moment it scrabbled with its claws, then slipped back into the lava with a terrible yowling cry.

"To the tunnel!" shouted Tanner, guiding Firepos toward the cavern entrance. A spatter of lava burst to one side, but the flame bird lifted a wing to stop it landing on him and sprang off the ground. Below, Nera pounced from rock to rock, and Falkor slithered around the edge of the cavern, gripping the stone with his powerful scales.

As Tanner reached the tunnel, Varlot leaped over a crack and landed across the entrance, standing defiantly in the way with his sword raised.

"If I die, we all die!" he bellowed.

Gwen soared past Tanner, kneeling on Gulkien's back. In a single move she grasped an ax and sent it spinning through the air. It slammed into the center of Varlot's forehead, embedding deep in the Beast's skull.

"Good shot!" called Castor.

For a moment, the Horse Beast's eyes rolled and he swayed on his feet.

"You know what to do!" Tanner said to Firepos.

With a screech, she shot a trailing fireball, enveloping Varlot's head in flames. Gor's Beast fell backward to the ground.

"You go first!" Tanner called to Rufus.

Falkor slithered over Varlot's smoldering corpse, followed by Nera, her golden fur slicked with sweat. Gulkien hovered for a moment, then plunged after them.

Tanner and Firepos flew over to Gor's creature — the horse that could morph into a warrior of frightening size. Tanner's first glimpse of Varlot had been terrifying, hooves that turned into massive fists, armor sliding over the horse's face as he reared up to stand. This creature could kill dozens of people with a few well-aimed punches or the vicious slice of a blade. Now he lay on his back, the weight of his own body pinning him to the ground as blood pooled around him. Fire flickered around the edges of his face as the armor melted to his flesh. His eyes gazed upward, unseeing.

"I wasn't sure we'd ever defeat you," Tanner called down. There was no response. Then he gave a start as the roof of the cavern collapsed in huge chunks of stone, and lava exploded in great fountains through the crater. Molten rock leaked across the floor from the hundreds of cracks. In the center Anoret stood proudly, watching the destruction and unmoved by the boulders that rained down on her.

"Come here, quick!" Tanner called. "I have something for you! Firepos, let me down." His Beast landed on a shallow ledge, and he scrabbled off her feathers.

Smoke swirled around Anoret as she strode toward him. He lifted the mask; the Beast gazed down at him, unblinking. Then, as though she understood, she lowered herself to a crouch as rocks fell around them.

Tanner leaped onto a boulder and turned the fused pieces of the mask around in his hand. He felt his fingers twitch, and his limbs felt as though they throbbed. He raised the mask above his head and a sudden energy seemed to spring through the air between Anoret and what was once her face. The mask flew out of Tanner's hands and with a flash of blinding light, morphed and spread over Anoret's skeletal features. Scars melted away and fresh skin blossomed across the Beast's cheekbones.

Thank you, came her voice.

She raised herself up, spreading her limbs and crying out in exultation. Anoret lifted a claw to Tanner. The cavern shook once more, and a huge section of the roof gave way. Then the Beast vanished behind a wall of smoke and debris.

Tanner leaped onto Firepos, and they raced through the gap. As they soared through the tunnel, Tanner realized they weren't clear of danger yet. Rock debris broke away around them, battering Tanner as he lay low against the flame bird's neck. He could feel her wings thudding up and down to get them to safety.

Finally, they burst out into the clear, cool air. Tanner guided Firepos in Gulkien's wake, toward the hillside, away from the plain. Nera and Falkor were already climbing the slope toward the remains of the Avantian army. As Tanner looked back he saw Derthsin's soldiers still manning the fortress walls, screaming and wailing as the structure collapsed around them. Above, lava erupted from the crater and burst from the side of the volcano. It poured down the mountainside, scorching everything in its path. Like some massive orange tongue, a river of molten rock rushed through the fortress gateway, coating the ramp and swallowing the soldiers at the bottom. With a rumble, the last of the fortress walls disintegrated into the moat.

Derthsin's stronghold was no more.

CHAPTER 13

Tanner landed Firepos beside Gulkien, and the flame bird shook the ash from her wings. Rufus was already working his way through the crowd of soldiers, using his magic to heal their injuries. As Tanner climbed stiffly from the flame bird's back, tired but elated, the crowd of soldiers let off a roar of triumph. He saw a few dozen smiling faces turned toward him.

We lost so many, he thought sadly.

The man called Raurk, with a bloodied bandage tied across his head, rushed to Tanner's side and gave him a mighty clap on the back.

"You did it!" he said.

"*We* did it," said Tanner.

Castor stood tall, balancing on Nera's back. "Avantia is free!" he shouted. The soldiers laughed and shouted back his words. Castor jumped down and joined a group of soldiers. "How many varkules did you kill?" he asked them. "There was one — a vicious brute with teeth as long as your forearm. He came at me from nowhere. . . ."

Gwen met Tanner's gaze and rolled her eyes. "Same old Castor." She smiled.

One by one, wiping their bloodied hands on their tunics, the survivors lined up to shake Tanner's hand. He took each one with a flood of gratitude.

"You're the hero of the battle," Gwen whispered teasingly in his ear.

Tanner shook his head. He knew he'd only done what he could. "Without all these people, we'd never even have gotten close to Derthsin," he said.

When Rufus had finished with the wounded soldiers, he tended to the Beasts. Firepos was unscathed after her miraculous resurrection, but Gulkien had numerous nicks in his delicate wings, and Gwen counted nine broken arrows shafts buried in his fur.

"He never even let on," she said proudly.

Castor went with one of the bands of soldiers to forage for food and firewood in the surrounding countryside. Rufus, meanwhile, turned his attentions to his own Beast. Patches of Falkor's scales had been scorched away, right through to the muscle in several patches, and he shimmered gold and bronze with gratitude as his rider healed the burns. Nera had a deep cut in her hind leg from a pike, and a tear in her cheek where a varkule had bitten her. She growled patiently as Rufus worked his magic and the wounds sealed up.

As darkness fell over the kingdom, the lava glowed brightly against the night. While some soldiers made camp, lighting fires and setting the cooking pots to boil, others took the task of digging graves for the dead. The raised mounds were silhouetted against the night, and the songs of victory were sung in mournful tones. Many fell asleep where they flopped to the ground, exhausted from the battle.

Tanner and his friends sat around their own small campfire with their Beasts. He'd told them about giving the mask back to Anoret.

"Did I do the right thing?" he asked them. "It felt right at the time."

Castor shrugged. "Oh yes. Fighting and killing for a mask that you then give away the first moment you can. That's a real hero's journey!" Tanner felt a muscle twitch in his jaw as he stared at his friend. Then Castor winked. "Only joking. Of course you did the right thing!"

Tanner shook his head slowly. "One day, Castor, I promise you . . ."

"What?" Castor asked, his eyes wide in mock shock. "Did I say something wrong?"

Gwen was laughing softly. "Will there ever be peace between you two?" she asked. Tanner and Castor were grinning at each other now.

"Never!" they both said at the same time. Rufus watched them all quietly. *Always watching*, Tanner thought. *Always assessing.*

Tanner looked up at the stars. His grandmother Esme had said they held the secret to the future, but for Tanner everything was uncertain. What other secrets lurked in the kingdom? What other enemies awaited them?

Avantia will need to be rebuilt, Tanner thought. *And the people who fought with us today have the strength to do it.*

Derthsin's cruelty would be remembered with terror for generations to come. The graves of those who had died would act as a painful reminder of all that had happened. But the spirit forged in Avantia's hour of need, by ordinary people coming together, would lay the foundations of a stronger kingdom.

Tanner shifted his aching body. For many years after his father's death, the worst day he had known was long hours in the heat of the bakery. Believing Derthsin already dead, he had yearned after the revenge he could never take. Gor's march into Forton that awful morning had shattered everything. It seemed long ago, not just a few weeks past, that Tanner had watched Gor stand over his grandmother's corpse, holding the sword still dripping with her blood. What would she make of him now, the boy who used to practice with a wooden sword in the vegetable garden? The enemy blood he had spilled would never make up for what he'd lost, but every drop was for her.

And what of his mother? Tanner tried to imagine what she'd been like: a small, pretty woman with long hair and eyes that burned with love for him. Tears swelled behind his eyes as he remembered the last time he saw her, her face split into a scream as Derthsin's men dragged her away. After everything that had happened, he could finally allow himself to hope that she was alive.

I'll find you, he murmured.

Tanner felt a smile spread across his lips. He let his eyes drift closed.

The following morning the sky was clear blue, aside from the plumes of ash drifting from the volcano's peak. The soldiers said their farewells, breaking camp and heading off in different directions to their villages.

Looking back toward the battlefield and the collapsed fortress beyond, Tanner felt no stirring of the old bloodlust within.

Gwen came to stand beside him.

"We achieved what we set out to do," she said. "Despite all the obstacles: Castor with his guilt, me with my grief for Geffen, Rufus and . . . well, his secret."

Rufus blushed. "Derthsin must have sensed I was susceptible," he muttered.

"What do you mean?" asked Castor.

The wizard boy sighed. "I've always known I had magical powers," he said, "but sometimes I wonder if I was born with a streak of weakness, too. I used my magic to show off sometimes."

Castor burst out laughing. "You're kidding? That's part of growing up. Look at me!"

Rufus chuckled nervously. "Maybe."

Gwen looked at Tanner. "What was your biggest challenge?" she asked.

Her question took him by surprise. Tanner thought through the previous days, from the death of his grandmother to the horror as he watched Firepos fall into the lava pit. There were so many things he could think of.

"Wearing the mask was my biggest challenge," he said. "The feeling when you wear it . . . the power within, the Beasts at your command. It's overwhelming."

The others watched him with concerned expressions, until a smile split Castor's face.

"Easy, then," he said. "Don't think about it anymore!"

Tanner forced himself to laugh. Firepos cawed softly to him. *This part of your journey is complete.*

Tanner walked over to the flame bird and stroked her gleaming feathers.

"What would I do without you?" he asked. She closed her eyes and pressed her body against his, the heat of her flesh warming him.

Gwen placed a hand on his shoulder.

"You've done all you set out to achieve — and more," she told him. Her eyes brimmed with tears, but the axes at her waist still sparkled dangerously.

"I'm only sorry . . ." Tanner couldn't complete the sentence. He didn't know how he could ever help Gwen forget her brother's tragic end.

"Don't worry," she said gently. "It's all right. Or it will be, one day."

Rufus's fingers twitched, as though he was impatient to use more magic. "Shouldn't we get going?" he asked.

Tanner turned to Firepos. "You've always been there for me," he said. "Since that first day in Forton when Derthsin came."

And I shall always be here, answered the Beast.

Placing a foot against Firepos's wing joint, he hoisted himself over her back. The others went to their Beasts.

"It's time for us to go home," Tanner said to the riders.

"I'll miss you," said Gwen, as Gulkien stretched out his wings. "And I know Geffen would, too."

Tanner blushed. "I won't be far away."

Falkor slithered to Firepos's side, and Rufus held out his hand. "I'm sorry, Tanner, about . . . you know . . ."

"Don't worry," said Tanner. "In a strange way, perhaps the Fates were guiding all of us. Derthsin wanted you to come to him, and if you hadn't, maybe none of us would have reached the cavern."

"*I* would have," muttered Castor. "You three were holding me up."

Then Castor's face opened into a wide smile, and they all laughed. Tanner nestled himself into Firepos's feathers. He had no idea what the future held for any of them, but he had a feeling they were bound together forever now. They all needed to return to where they came from, but for how long? When would they see one another again? There was still much to do if Avantia was to be returned to the kingdom it once was. But for now . . .

"Take me home," he said, and Firepos rose into the air.

I spread my phoenix wings, stronger than ever with the volcano's magic. Lifting my head, I open my beak and call to the others with a cry that echoes through the still morning air. I leap into the sky and climb quickly.

Your work here is done, Tanner. We have fought off Derthsin and the pieces of the mask are returned to Anoret, mother to us all.

But for every piece of good fortune, there is an opposite. Today the sky is clear, but the storm clouds will return. I sense a new, unknown path before us. Where it will lead, the Fates shall decide.

For now, though, I push these brooding thoughts away. I have my friends beside me — the Beasts I was born with. Gulkien tips his head and howls with joy. Falkor tastes the peaceful air with his tongue. Nera springs with the step of a Beast who savors victory.

My friends, this fight is over, but others will come. We may be parted, but I shall call you to me again some day.

And we will come, *they reply.*

And Tanner. My brave rider. The one I chose, or who was chosen for me. Always Tanner.

No one will part us, my Chosen One. Together we will face whatever Destiny puts in our way.

AN UNLIKELY HERO
ARISES . . .

THE CHRONICLES OF
AVANTIA

1 FIRST HERO

SEE HOW THE QUEST FOR
AVANTIA BEGAN. . . .

Angry skies and the clash of swords filled Tanner's dreams. A harsh cry sounded out and he felt himself being torn from sleep, rushing up to the surface of consciousness. His eyelashes fluttered open. He realized that the cry that woke him had come from his own lips. Moonlight flooded through the window. He sat up and dragged a weary hand across his eyes. His dream lingered in his thoughts, threatening and deadly.

With a sigh, he threw off his blankets and scrambled out of bed, wincing as his feet touched the cold floor. He pushed his long hair out of his eyes and splashed cold water from a tin basin onto his face. Feeling more awake, he pulled his tunic over his head and tugged on his battered old boots.

He looked out of the window. Light gathered on the horizon, glowing on the rough track that led to Forton. To the north, in the direction of Harron, he saw a faint orange glow. *A bonfire, perhaps?* Tanner wondered. He gazed at his reflection in the dirty windowpane. Long brown hair framed his pale face. Above high cheekbones, his dark eyes betrayed last night's troubled sleep.

I'm late for work, he thought. No time for breakfast. He creeped past his grandmother's room and smiled as he heard her soft snores. Quietly opening the front door, he stepped into the cold morning. The air misted as he took a few deep breaths. Tanner smelled mint drifting from the well-tended herb garden. The plants had been crushed by something large, and some of the leaves were charred at the edges. "That won't make Grandmother very happy," he muttered, smiling. He knew who the culprit was!

His route to the bakery in Forton where he worked led down the path behind a row of thatched cottages, not far from the edge of the woods where his father had been killed and his mother abducted. It was hard to believe that eight years had passed since that terrible day. The memory of it was as raw as ever: the anguish of his dying father's face, his mother's screams as she was dragged away.

Tanner shook his head and ran to the bakery.

Heat blasted over Tanner's body as he sucked in the scorching air. Sweat poured off him, even though he was stripped to the waist. Although not yet fully grown, Tanner was lithe, nimble, and stronger than he looked.

Using the long-handled paddle, he took the last loaves from the oven and laid them to rest on the cooling racks. He put a couple of loaves under his arm, waved good-bye to the baker — who still had a day of selling bread ahead of him — and stepped into Forton's village square. In the hours since he'd started work, it had filled with people. The sun had risen over the rooftops, and shutters were opening to the smell of fresh bread.

Tanner stood for a moment, raising his face to the sun. A washerwoman hurried past with bundles of clean linen under her arms. A fisherman and his son, Ben, balanced a pole strung with trout across their shoulders.

"Stop by our stall later," Ben called to Tanner. "I'll have some fried fish for you, in exchange for bread."

Tanner grinned at Ben and lifted a hand in acknowledgment. After the loss of his parents, he had thought there was nothing to live for, but time had gone some way to heal the wound. He had many friends in the village. And his grandmother, although grumpy and short-tempered, looked after him. *Life could be worse*, he always told himself, when he felt sad.

Tanner looked at the stout wooden palisade topped with sharpened stakes, and at the shallow, dry moat surrounding Forton. Defenses had been added when Forton was rebuilt after Derthsin's attack. Despite the protection, fear of violence remained — Avantia was a dangerous place, with no ruler. War bands roamed the lands, raiding villages, and bandits prowled the quieter stretches of road.

MORE FROM ADAM BLADE

DIVE DEEP INTO